The Tour Guide
A Psychological Thri
Copyright, 2025
All Rights Reserved
Nash Greene

Table of Contents
About the book

Chapter One

Chapter Two

Chapter Three

Chapter Four

Chapter Five

Chapter Six

Chapter Seven

Chapter Eight

Chapter Nine

Chapter Ten

Chapter Eleven

Chapter Twelve

Chapter Thirteen

Chapter Fourteen

Chapter Fifteen

Chapter Sixteen

Chapter Seventeen

Chapter Eighteen

Chapter Nineteen

Chapter Twenty

Chapter Twenty-One

Chapter Twenty-Two

Chapter Twenty-Three

Chapter Twenty-Four

Chapter Twenty-Five

Chapter Twenty-Six

Chapter Twenty-Seven

Chapter Twenty-Eight

Chapter Twenty-Nine

Chapter Thirty

Chapter Thirty-One

Chapter Thirty-Two

Chapter Thirty-Three

Chapter Thirty-Four

Chapter Thirty-Five

Chapter Thirty-Six

Chapter Thirty-Seven

Chapter Thirty-Eight

Chapter Thirty-Nine

Chapter Forty

Chapter Forty-One

Chapter Forty-Two

Chapter Forty-Three

Chapter Forty-Four

Chapter Forty-Five

Chapter Forty-Six

Chapter Forty-Seven

Chapter Forty-Eight

Chapter Forty-Nine

Chapter Fifty

Chapter Fifty-One

Chapter Fifty-Two

Chapter Fifty-Three

About the book

What started as a picturesque family vacation to New York City has turned into every parent's worst nightmare for Bruce and Judy Hurt.

A man claimed to be their tour guide.

But he wasn't.

And now their daughter has been kidnapped for ransom.

Bruce and Judy imagined this being a week they would always remember, but not like this. Not as a horrific nightmare.

And sometimes nightmares come back.

Chapter One
Judy

This feels like it is going to be a perfect family vacation where nothing bad happens. I've felt that way ever since sitting down in the plane, and now I feel it even more after arriving at our destination.

I hope I'm not wrong about that.

The New York skyline glimmers through the windows of JFK airport as snow falls heavily from the dark gray sky. My husband Bruce stands at my side and smiles at me as we hold hands and gaze out at Manhattan.

"I'm glad you talked me into taking some time off from work. This is going to be special," he says, glancing at me out of the corner of his eye as a smile curls up on his face.

"And I'm glad you finally relented," I say.

Bruce chuckles and leans in to peck me gently on the cheek. He knows how much I've been wanting him to take some time off from running his corporation. He's a workaholic and I won't lie; it's been an immense strain on our marriage over the last year. Agreeing to take a family vacation to New York for an entire week was an incredibly pleasant and shocking surprise, although I knew he'd have never offered it on his own. It took me bringing up the idea for him to even consider it.

"Mom, it's New York!" Annie beams at us from below and hops excitedly up and down. Bruce reaches down and hoists her up over his shoulder. She giggles and peers out through the window.

"Here's a better vantage point, sweetie."

"What's a vantage point?" She asks.

"It means view point, sweetie – from up high here on Daddy's shoulder you'll have a better view," Bruce says.

Annie stretches her arms out and grins from ear to ear. "Wow. It's a huge city. It's bigger than San Francisco!"

"A lot bigger than San Francisco, sweetie." Bruce nods and brings her back down to ground level, dropping her gently on the floor and patting her on the head. "Now, are you ready to go have some fun in New York City?"

"Yes. Do we get pizza later?"

"Of course we do! We're in New York, after all. What's a trip to New York without trying out the famous pizza?"

Annie smiles and looks back out the window excitedly. She is eleven years old and the best thing that has ever happened to me. She has been a blessing to us in so many ways and has brought us closer over the years. Whenever we happen to argue, the one thing that seems to truly help is remembering the sweet girl we brought into this world together.

And it isn't as if we argue *that* frequently, but over the last year, Bruce's passion for his job has simply gone overboard. I'm hoping that the decision to take this family trip is a sign that he is going to reign in some of the excess work and spend more time at home. We have enough money as it is and Bruce knows this, but he can't seem to stop spending the majority of his waking hours in his office. It's like an addiction.

As for myself, I run a small personal training business, operating out of a small studio in downtown San Francisco. I have about twenty clients I work with throughout the week and that gives me a lot of downtime. I'm grateful for it. It's a profession I'm passionate about, and yet it doesn't take over my life. I have so much time to be with our daughter – and Bruce, whenever he actually manages to come home before I'm already asleep.

"Come on, girls," he says cheerfully, taking me gently by the arm and leading the way through the busy airport. As I hold onto Annie's little hand tightly, we zig-zag through the thousands of people as we make our way to the exit. As soon as the doors open, the crisp, wintry air smacks us in the face and it reminds me of how much I appreciate weather on the West Coast. Although I grew up in the Northeast, I was never able to get used to the frigid winters, and moving to California for college made me realize that I was meant to live in mild climates.

Still, there is something deeply nostalgic about feeling the cold early December wind swirling all around us as we stand in line waiting for a taxi, and I'm brought back to the days of my youth spent playing outside in the snow with all the other children in my neighborhood. I look down at Annie and rub her head. She's got on her mittens and puffy winter jacket, and she looks as toasty as she can be while she stands close to me, clutching my hand shyly and glancing this way and that with the wide, curious eyes of a child observing new surroundings.

I keep a watchful eye on her, being the protective mother that I am. Although I know we are in a relatively safe city, all things considered. Still, *no* city is one hundred percent safe, and I can't help but feel like I need to keep my eye on her, just in case. I don't know what I would do if something were to happen to Annie.

Of course, I'm sure that nothing will, and so I know that it's a silly thing to be worrying about. This is going to be a wonderful trip for the three of us, and I hope it will serve as a sort of fresh start for Bruce and me. Perhaps it will bring us closer together, like we used to be. We used to be so young and in love.

As we reach the front of the line, a cab driver hops out and helps us with our luggage. The three of us crawl into the warm cab and close the doors shut. A moment later we are moving, bound for the city. The snow still hasn't stopped falling; if anything it has grown in intensity, and it covers the streets and the sidewalks as the taxi cab plows through it steadily, taking us across the Queensborough Bridge. The Manhattan skyline looms up ahead, blanketed in snow.

"It's a big city," Annie exclaims, staring up ahead with wide eyes.

"It sure is," Bruce says. "We're going to have some fun this week, aren't we, girls?" He glances back at us from the front passenger seat and winks.

"Yep. I can't wait to eat yummy pizza," Annie says excitedly.

I rub her head and smile. I think that Bruce is right. We're going to have a lot of fun this week.

This is truly going to be a wonderful trip, isn't it?

Chapter Two
Bruce

After checking in to the two bedroom suite on the forty-second floor, the three of us lie in bed for a few minutes to recharge our batteries. It was a longer than usual trip from San Francisco, with a two hour delay before boarding, but now we've made it and I feel ready to go out and face the seasonal crowds of Christmas shoppers, commuters heading home after a long day at the office, and of course out-of-towners like us; tourists from all over the world.

The last time I was in New York was for a business trip. Actually, the last *several* times I was in New York were business trips. In fact, I can't quite remember the last time I was here for pleasure. It has been a long time.

After freshening up a bit, we head outside and walk around the urban winter wonderland. Snowflakes plummet endlessly from the darkening sky. The moon pokes out through the clouds and becomes full, shining down on Manhattan as taxis honk and pedestrians scurry across the crosswalks, trudging through the crunchy snow.

It's a gorgeous evening, and it brings me back to what I miss the most about living in New York – the winter! I'm a fan of snow, especially in the city, oddly enough. Sure, after less than half a day it tends to look like an ugly shade of gray, but a fresh snowfall over Manhattan makes the city look just about as beautiful as any of the modern wonders of the world.

Call me crazy, but that's how I feel, and as we stroll down West 34th Street I keep glancing down at Annie to see what the expression on her face looks like. Each time I do, I see that she's got big, bulbous eyes. The lights of the city are reflected in her big pupils as she stares up at the snow-covered concrete jungle with seeming awe. It gives me, a middle-aged man, the sense that I'm looking at the city for the first time through my daughter's eyes. It makes the whole experience so much more special.

"I'm getting awfully hungry. What about you two?" Judy says as we approach 9th Avenue. We're right at the edge of the neighborhood known as Hell's Kitchen. Despite its name, it's a desirable and pricy Midtown neighborhood, and fortunately for my hungry wife, it has lots of delicious restaurants.

"I could go for something as well. If I'm remembering correctly, there's a great Italian restaurant several blocks north of us. Hank Fredericks and I went there twice during that last business trip. Great wine. Amazing sangria. And of course good food as well," I add with a smile.

Judy looks down at Annie. "Does Italian sound good to you?"

"They've got pizza, don't they?" Annie beams up at us as snowflakes trickle down on her rosy cheeks.

"I'd say so, and I bet it tastes pretty good." I nod, giving her a little wink.

"Okay. Sounds good to me."

The three of us trudge through the heavy snow. There must be nearly a foot of it, and the forecasters are calling for another seven or eight inches tonight. It won't keep us from getting outdoors, though. Annie has been talking all month about wanting to see Central Park, and I think with this amount of snowfall it will feel so tranquil and nice. We'll have to head there early, though, and then take the train back down to our hotel on 39th Street before ten a.m., because that's when our tour guide is meeting us.

A tour guide for a town I've spent plenty of time in seems a bit silly, I know, but I thought it would be fun for Annie and Judy, and maybe they'll be able to take us to some neat spots that most people don't know about. Besides, I mentioned to them in the email that I'd like to see some things around the West Village and the Financial District if possible, since those are two neighborhoods I haven't spent a whole lot of time in during my business trips here. The company wrote back and said that it would be no problem, and that they knew every block of the city like the back of their hand. That's a bit hard to believe, but we'll find out tomorrow, I suppose. They're supposedly going to give us a tour that lasts about seven hours, so by the time we're finished I think Annie will be ready for a long night's sleep back at the hotel.

Luckily for us, the Italian restaurant I mentioned is right where I remembered it being, and as I hold the door open for Annie and Judy they hurry in before me. Stepping into the warm, cozy little hole in the wall restaurant feels so pleasant on a frigid day like today. The owner seats us at a small, intimate table in the back corner and hands us three menus.

Judy and I order pasta, while Annie of course orders pizza. She drinks her orange juice happily while Judy and I toast our wine glasses together and stare into each other's eyes. I feel good about this trip, and I'm happy that she talked me into it. I know I've been working far too much in the last year or two, but I aim to change that soon. I think that this week is going to be perfect.

In fact, I have a feeling that this will be a week none of us ever forget.

Chapter Three
Annie

I have always wanted to go to New York ever since I was a little kid and saw it on TV. Now that I'm bigger I'm glad Dad finally brought Mom and me. I think if he had brought me when I was a little kid I might have been scared of how tall the buildings are, and how many people there are in places like Times Square. I know that San Francisco is a big town, but that's my hometown and I'm used to it, and besides, it's definitely not as big as *this* place. Holy cow, I can't believe how many people are walking around on the sidewalks, and how many taxis there are. And bicycles! They ride bikes here so fast, zig zagging through cars. I'd be way too scared to try that. Not that Dad would let me, of course. And I don't think even Mom would let me try.

The nice man that works here at the restaurant brings us our food. I don't know what Mom and Dad ordered – some kind of pasta, I guess – but I ordered pizza, of course, because I always wanted to try New York pizza. San Francisco has some really good pizza, but I know that New York pizza is supposed to be amazing from what Dad has told me. Hopefully this place is as good as he acted like it would be.

I close my eyes and take a bite. It's hot! I grab my glass and quickly wash it down without getting much of a chance to enjoy the taste, but even with the first bite being quick and scalding hot, I can tell it's amazing. I blow on the slice a little, trying to cool it down, and then I take another bite – this one more careful than the first. Then I feel the flavor erupt on my tastebuds. Holy moly, it's amazing! I can't stop smiling as I eat the pizza. I try to eat it slowly, but it's so good I can't seem to stop taking big bites.

"You gonna share a piece of that with your sweet dad?" Dad looks down at me with a sad, puppy-dog look to his eyes. Before I can get a chance to answer, he waves his hand and giggles. "I'm just joking, sweetheart. You enjoy that pizza. Want some pasta?"

"No thanks." I shake my head and reach for another slice of pizza. "Sure you don't want some? Mom?"

They both shake their heads. More for me, then. I wouldn't mind sharing a slice with each of them, but I'm more than happy to eat it all by myself. In fact, that sounds perfect to me, considering I'm probably the world's biggest pizza lover.

I start the second slice and lean back in my seat. "It's *so* good!"

My parents laugh as they sip wine and watch me eating like a big goofball, sitting there with a big smile on my face and googly eyes as I finish off the second slice and start on the third.

So far, this trip is awesome, and it's only just the beginning.

Chapter Four
Judy

What a wonderful night's sleep that was. I feel refreshed as I sit up in bed and slide my legs out from under the sheets. I walk slowly over to the window, draw the blinds, and immediately feel myself squinting from the brightness. There must have been quite a bit more snowfall overnight, because the city is coated in a layer of it, and everything looks as white as a new sheet of paper. Gone is the dirty New York sludge we trekked through last night on our way back to the hotel. I have to admit, I found it a bit challenging, dodging big puddles of brown half-frozen water and massive mounds of dirty snow up by the edges of the sidewalk.

It looks beautiful now, though, and I wonder how long it'll last. Not long, I'm sure. I think it would be a shame not to take advantage of it while it's still clean and beautiful. I check my watch. It's six o'clock. I think I'll go ahead and wake up Bruce and Annie now, but as I turn to do so I see that Bruce is already awake and sitting on the edge of the bed, rubbing his eyes sleepily as he yawns.

"Morning," he says.

"Good morning. Sleep well?"

"Yeah, how about you?"

"I slept great. This room gets so dark with the blackout curtains. Let's wake this little sleepyhead and head up to Central Park. That was the plan, right?"

"Yes, let's head there early and get back here before ten o'clock. That's when the tour guide is supposed to come." He pauses, yawning again, and then adds, "Hopefully that wasn't a stupid idea."

"What?" I say.

"Hiring a tour guide. The company had good reviews, but I mean, I know this city."

"Oh, it'll be fun. You've been here on business, Bruce. You don't know Manhattan all that well."

"I guess you're right." He smiles and gets up out of bed, stretching his arms out in the air before going over to fix some coffee.

We have breakfast delivered by room service a while later, and then we take a cab to Central Park and spend the next couple of hours exploring in the snow. It's truly serene and feels magical, wandering around the nearly empty park with so much untouched snowfall covering it. Annie has a wonderful time spent laughing, playing, running around, making snow angels, and building snowmen. I'm glad she got to experience this, and I wish we could spend more time here together, but it's already a few minutes after nine, and that means it's time for us to make our way back to the hotel so that we can get into some dry clothes before our tour guide arrives.

Bruce takes a quick shower as Annie and I stand looking out the window. She points at numerous buildings and landmarks and asks me all about them. I have to chuckle and tell her that I probably know just as little as she knows about most of the buildings. Of course, I'm able to tell her what certain famous landmarks are: the Empire State Building, for instance. I tell her we can go up to the top sometime during the week if the weather permits. She smiles and nods, looking visibly excited at the idea.

Bruce comes out of the bathroom straightening his collar and smiles. He checks his watch. "Okay, it's about time. You two ready? Let's head down to the lobby to meet the tour guide."

"Ready, Daddy," Annie says.

He gives her a big thumbs up before throwing on his coat. We follow him out into the hallway and ride the elevator down. When we reach the lobby, we sit facing the front doors and stare out at the bustling sidewalk. Bruce keeps checking his watch. Ten o'clock rolls around. Another five minutes pass. Then another.

"Completely unprofessional," Bruce murmurs gruffly, rising to his feet. "I say we just call and cancel with the company. I'll insist on a refund due to them being late. A tour guide company shouldn't-"

"Mr. Hurt? Bruce Hurt? I'm Tony, your tour guide." A young man stands behind him, small with dusty blonde hair and a very thin freckled face. His bright eyes suggest he is in his late teens or early twenties at the most, although from some angles he looks younger, which is a bit startling considering he is our tour guide. The suit he wears looks about two sizes too large and the watch on his wrist slides around as he wipes sweat from his brow with a gloved hand. He looks a bit disoriented for a moment. That, or simply nervous.

He extends a hand and smiles sheepishly, "I'm so sorry, sir. I went into the wrong side of the lobby, I guess." He pauses for a moment. "This hotel's really big and it's kind of confusing."

"It's alright," Bruce says, shaking the man's hand. He seems to have calmed down a bit as he turns to me and shrugs with a look on his face that says: *Okay, I guess let's just go through with this since the guy's here now. No sense in cancelling now. Maybe I got a little flustered too quickly.*

I know that look all too well. Bruce turns back to the man and says, "How old are you? You hardly look old enough to be driving." He chuckles.

"I'm nineteen, I just look younger," the man quickly replies, chuckling a little.

"Alright, just making sure you've got your license," Bruce jokes.

"Yeah, I understand that, sir. My dad's got a baby face too. He said he still got carded for booze when he was thirty-five. Can you believe that?"

The thin young man comes around past Bruce and extends his hand towards me. "And you must be Mrs. Hurt. It's a pleasure to meet you."

We shake hands and I smile. "Nice to meet you."

Then, noticing Annie, his grin widens and he squats down a bit to meet her at eye level. He tilts his head to the side playfully. "And who's this young lady?"

"This is our daughter, Annie."

"First time in New York, Annie?"

"Yes," she says shyly, peeking out from behind my leg.

"Well, I'll tell you what. We'll make sure the four of us have some big fun today! How's that sound?"

Annie doesn't answer. Rising back up, Tony stands there with the merry grin still spread across his gaunt face as he looks at Bruce and me. "So, what spots in New York would you all like to check out? I know some good places of my own, but we can hit a lot of different locations since we've got all day."

"I mentioned the Financial District in my email. It was just an idea, though. We're kind of open to anything."

"Okay. You're a businessman, aren't you, Mr. Hurt?"

"Sure am. Call me Bruce."

"Mind if I ask what you do, Bruce? Sorry to pry, I'm just always motivated hearing other people's success stories, and I hope you don't mind if I say you appear to be a very successful man."

"Oh yeah?" Bruce chuckles, blushing a little. "Uh, well, my story isn't really all that interesting. I'm an investor, mostly. Nothing too exciting, to be honest."

"Cool, very cool," the man says, but his eyes show a lack of interest. They swivel around slowly past Bruce and stop at my face. For a second I feel very uncomfortable with the look he is giving me, but I don't know if it's just my imagination.

A moment later, as if noticing my discomfort, Tony looks down at the ground before looking back up at Bruce. "Okay then, let's get going. I'm sorry again about being a few minutes late." He points towards the hotel doors. "My car's out front."

We ride through the snowy Midtown streets towards downtown. I think we're on Broadway, but I'm not sure. For a tour guide, Tony has been awfully quiet ever since we left the hotel, but maybe he's focused on driving. Considering the wintry road conditions, I'm actually quite grateful for that. After a while, he looks in the rearview mirror at us, his eyes twinkling with curiosity.

"So, you folks don't know New York very well?"

Bruce opens his mouth and starts to speak, then pauses for a moment, as if trying to find the words. He chuckles and says, "I was going to say I know it pretty well, but that's just my ego talking." He glances over at me and smiles humbly, then turns his eyes back towards Tony. "The truth is that I've only really spent time here on business for the most part, so I never really got to explore the city much."

"Gotcha. Well, I'll show you the ropes. By the end of the day you'll all be like natives. Trust me." Tony flashes a smile at us in the mirror.

"How long have you lived in New York, Tony?" Bruce asks.

"All my life. Cant ya tell from my accent?" He grins again.

We chuckle. I peer down at Annie and say, "You excited for some sightseeing in the snow?"

She nods up at me, smiling, and says, "I liked making snow angels today. That was so fun. Mom, can we go back there later?"

"I think you'll be wiped out later, and I'm sure Dad and I will be. But we'll see. Maybe tonight we'll have another little Central Park adventure."

She looks giddy, but I meant it when I said I think the three of us will be exhausted later, because I know how Annie gets after a long day of sightseeing, and I highly doubt she will be up for going out tonight. If my prediction is right, she'll be sound asleep in the hotel bed by seven thirty or eight, or whenever we finish dinner. Speaking of which, I wonder what the plans are for tonight.

"What are the plans for dinner?" I ask Bruce.

"I figured we'd find something near the hotel. Tomorrow night I made a reservation for us at Mark's Steakhouse. It's supposed to be some of the best beef in the city. They've got a menu for kids, too." He glances down at Annie.

"Do they have nuggets and cheeseburgers?"

"You better believe it, honey," Bruce says. "Before your old man makes a reservation anywhere, he always makes sure they've got chicken nuggets and cheeseburgers on the menu." He chuckles, rubbing her head playfully. She giggles and pushes his hand away.

"No you don't."

"I sure do," he says in a defiant, lighthearted voice.

Tony clears his throat from the front of the car. "We'll park downtown and then I'll show you all around the Financial District. I know some very good spots I think you might be interested in, Mr. Hurt – sorry, I mean Bruce. You know, since you're a successful businessman and all."

"That sounds nice, Tony. Thanks. Hopefully the girls won't be bored." He chuckles and pokes me teasingly on the shoulder. "After looking at the financial district, you might be able to think of a place a little more exciting for my wife. She likes to shop."

"Soho is the place for that," Tony says, pointing a finger in the air. "They've got all sorts of clothing stores. Fancy stuff, mid-range stuff. All sorts of stuff." He smiles.

"Sounds good," I say. I wasn't planning on doing much shopping, but maybe checking out the shops would be fun on a snowy day like today. At least it would be a welcome break from being outdoors on this chilly day with the snow crunching under our feet.

We take a swift right and barrel down a snowy side street. Up in the driver's seat, Tony glances back at us in the rearview mirror. He is no longer smiling, and in fact looks quite serious as he gazes at me. Then he looks away before taking another series of turns and brings us back out onto a big, broad street, continuing our ride down towards the Financial District. At least, I think that's the direction we're heading, but I feel like I'm starting to get a bit mixed up.

Regardless, it all seems to work out in the end. About fifteen minutes later we pull into a parking structure and drive up to the third level. "Here we are. We'll walk the rest of the way," Tony says as he pulls into a spot. He gets out first and quickly hurries to the back doors before Bruce and I get a chance to open them. He swings them open for us and holds an arm out. "Hope the ride wasn't too bumpy for you, folks."

Bruce gets out and then Annie and I begin to slide out behind him.

But then the door slams shut before I get a chance to even get my foot out of it.

I stare with sudden confusion and a growing sense of horror when I realize that Tony, the driver, has shut the door intentionally and is staring at me with a menacing gaze from where he stands beside my daughter. My heart starts to jackhammer with fear when I see Annie turning and looking at me through the glass. She is smiling. She doesn't know that anything is wrong. For all she knows, I'm playing a silly game. But then her smile fades and she looks worried. Bruce, hands in his pockets, has his back to us. He hasn't noticed that anything has happened yet.

"*Bruce!*" I scream as I try to unlock the door.

The lock won't budge. I can't get the door open.

I can't get out of here.

Bruce turns, giving me a confused look. Then his eyes narrow as he points from Tony to me in the car. "You going to open the door for my wife, pal? She's stuck in there." He sounds slightly annoyed, thinking it's just a little accident. Tony says nothing.

"I said are you going to let my wife out of the car? Come on, this is ridiculous." Bruce walks over to the car and grabs the handle. It won't open. He turns back to Tony, who is staring straight ahead with his back to us. "Unlock the door, Tony. What are you doing, man?" He pauses. "I said *unlock the door*."

His eyes grow wide as he turns to me again and stares in through the window. He tries the door again, jerking on it frantically before he turns and looks at Tony. "Open the door. *OPEN the door – NOW!*" He shouts. Beside him, Annie has begun to sniffle nervously. I bang on the glass and start to yell, hoping someone can hear.

But the garage seems empty.

Tony, checking his watch, says nothing. Then he reaches into his pocket and pulls out what looks like some kind of small gun or taser.

Spinning methodically on his feet, he aims the object and then seems to fire it at Bruce, who quickly lets out a stifled gasp and collapses to his knees. It is a taser – I've seen them used before, but only in videos. I scream and start to bang harder on the glass as Annie spins her head back and forth between me, trapped in the car, and her father, lying twitching on the ground. Tony grabs him and puts a rag over his face. I watch as Bruce goes completely limp from whatever chemical he has just inhaled.

A van suddenly turns the corner and coasts quickly up in our direction before pulling smoothly into a parking spot two spaces down from ours. I bang on the windows harder, screaming so loud that my throat feels raw.

A man emerges from the van. A second later I watch as he and Tony grab Annie by the arms and lead her towards the van. Opening the back door, the man pushes her up into it and then slams the doors shut. Tony turns and leers at me from where I sit in the back seat of his car screaming. I'm alternating between slamming my fists on the window and trying the handle. It's useless.

I'm trapped in here.

And they have my precious baby.

Tony appears at the window and leans down so that his face is nearly pressed up against it. The glass fogs as he speaks slowly, calmly: "If you call the police, your daughter will die. If you try to hire anyone to find us, your daughter will die. If you tell any friends or family, your daughter will die. I am not bluffing you." He pauses, giving me an icy gaze. "If you want your child, you and your husband will pay the sum of one million dollars. It is a fair price for her life, and any attempt to negotiate will be met with a bitter end for your daughter. You will receive further instructions from us this evening at your hotel." He pauses again to glare at me, then he says slowly, "If you tell the police or anyone else, she will die, and you will live with that guilt for the rest of your life. I am going to unlock the door now. Do not move until we are out of sight."

He holds the key fob near his face and presses it, unlocking the doors. Then he turns and struts off. Bruce rises from the ground and tries to reach for him but then falls back down onto his knees and catches himself with his hands. Tony gets into the passenger side of the van, slams the door shut, and then it pulls out of the spot and speeds off. I hear its tires squeaking as it turns quickly during the descent down each level of the garage. Then there is silence.

Chapter Five
Bruce

"I'm going to be sick," I stammer as I rush over to the edge of the parking garage and start to gag. I don't know what he put over my mouth, but whatever it was it knocked me out cold and made me feel like I've got the worst hangover of my life.

But that isn't what I'm concerned about now. I turn and stumble back over to Judy, who looks shellshocked. My first thought was to call the police, but as soon as I pulled my phone from my pocket Judy warned me against that, telling me what the driver had told her.

Was he bluffing?

I can't risk finding out.

I turn and see Judy standing there, looking just as hopeless as me, if not more so. Neither of us have a clue what to do. This isn't something I thought happened in real life. Situations like this are reserved for weekly crime episodes on television, not real life. This has to be a dream. I'm sleeping now, aren't I? I'm tossing and turning in the king sized bed on the forty-second floor, and any minute now I'm going to wake up and take a big breath and say: *'Well, that was one silly dream and I'm glad it's over.'*

I wish that were the case, but I know it's not.

Because I know this isn't a dream. A dream couldn't possibly feel this intense, this *physical.* There's no mistaking the sensation of my heart lurching in my chest, feeling as if it is on the verge of bursting through my ribcage. For the very first time in my life, I feel completely useless.

"He's got to be bluffing," I say, pulling my phone out and pressing the first number. Judy grabs the phone from my hand before I have a chance to dial the remaining two numbers. I stand there staring at her, mouth agape, hands shaking. "We've got to call the police," I say. "There is no other alternative."

"I told you what they said. They said they'd kill her if we went to the police. Do you understand that, Bruce? They'll kill our baby girl." Her voice shakes as tears fill her eyes. I've never seen my wife look so panic stricken.

I guess she is right. What was I *thinking*? I could have gotten Annie killed. I guess it's just a natural reaction, though, because what else could I do in a situation like this? Call the tour guide company and ask them to give my daughter back? Maybe if I'm real nice about it and say 'pretty please' they won't be able to resist.

I feel nauseous and feverish with fear.

Because by now it's apparent that the company is fake. It must be. The reviews must have been fake; the whole thing must have been elaborately set up to ensnare wealthy couples like Judy and myself and then extort them. That's what I figure, at least. But how legitimate are their threats? Have they done this before, or are we the first suckers who fell into their trap?

Judy is right. It's not worth finding out if they're bluffing. Maybe we'd call the cops and they'd have no idea. Or maybe they've got eyes on us somehow and will find out. Maybe they are watching us now, somehow. Then they'll kill Annie. God, the thought makes me shudder. It makes my stomach feel queasy, and I'm so glad that Judy snatched the phone from my hand before I got a chance to contact the police.

"They want one million dollars." Her voice trembles as she gazes at me gravely. "We'll give it to them. I'd give them everything we have. Our house, our possessions, the clothes on our back. Everything. Money means nothing compared to Annie."

Sirens suddenly wail from somewhere close. Red and blue lights flash down below us on a lower level. A police cruiser twists around the curve and races in our direction, then the wheels skid on the pavement as the car comes screeching to a halt. Two officers emerge from the car, hands positioned on their holsters.

"Get your hands up! *Get them up!*" One of them shouts.

This has to be some kind of horrible dream.
It has to be.

"What's the deal? You got a problem with the lady? You think you're a big man up here bullying her?" The same cop spits on the ground and glares at me as he approaches, cocking his head to the side and looking at me like I'm scum of the earth.

"What? What are you talking about?" I stammer. "Listen, Officer, my-"

"Shut up." He scowls at me, sizing me up with his beady eyes. "We got reports of screaming from a man parking his car on the level below." He turns to Judy and says in a soft, but stern voice, "Ma'am, are you okay? Was this man trying to hurt you?"

My head is spinning, and I can't understand what is happening. I feel dizzy, like I've been drugged, but it's just the adrenaline coursing through me.

Judy doesn't say anything, but she shakes her head. Her protruding eyes make her look shellshocked, and I guess the officer thinks she's shaken up because of *me*. She just keeps shaking her head, staring off into space, opening her mouth to speak but stopping before any words come out. I can tell she is thinking the same thing I am – *should we tell them*?

The cop turns to me as his partner keeps a close watch on Judy, and he says angrily, "Let me see some ID. Don't make me ask again. Looks like you got this lady all rattled up and scared to talk."

"It's not that," I say.

"*Shut up*," he says, waving a finger.

I tighten my lips together and pull out my ID. I have two cousins who are police officers. They're wonderful people, and I wish they were here to back me up at this moment. But they're far off in Santa Cruz, California, and I know they're no help to me here as I stand face to face with this bully on a power trip. But then again, is he really a bully? After all, he thinks I was hurting Judy, and I guess neither of us have convinced him otherwise. We're both acting awkward right now because of what's just happened to us – and because of the fact that we can't tell him.

What do we do?

I hand him my ID and he looks at it. "Tourists. Didn't need to see your ID to figure that. Could tell from the accent." He glances back up at me and smirks as he hands me back my driver's license. "You want to tell me what the screaming was about? That boy who called in sounded awfully scared, from what I heard. Heard bloodcurdling screams. I don't take kindly to men who treat women badly, but I also don't take kindly to liars, so be straight with me. No more games."

"That's my wife. I'd never hurt her."

He glances back at Judy who has sunk down to the ground. She is visibly distraught, and I can't blame her. God knows the horrible things she is thinking right now – probably the same things I'm thinking. Terrifying thoughts about what might happen to our daughter. What if we never see her again? God, what if they really *kill* her?

"Her eyes say otherwise. She looks traumatized," the cop says, turning back to me with a livid scowl.

"They took her," Judy blurts out. "Two men took our daughter. They kidnapped her. Please, for the love of God, help us. They told us we can't contact the police, or they'll kill her, but now…" She pauses, holding her hand up as she waves it at the officers. "It looks like we don't have much of a choice now, do we?"

"Whoa, whoa. Back up. What? What are you talking – *who* took your daughter?"

I groan and rub my face. Every second that passes is a precious second wasted, lost.

A second that could mean everything for our daughter.

"A tour guide. I mean, he *said* he was a tour guide," Judy says.

"Wait, what tour guide? What happened?" He looks at both of us, shifting his eyes back and forth.

"Officer," I say frantically, cutting him off as I point at the car behind me. "Listen, the man driving this car claimed to be from a tour guide company – the name of the company I forget, but I can check the email on my phone; it's all there – and listen, this man *took our daughter*. For Christ's sake, he took our *daughter*, and I don't know what to do to get her back, and I-"

Judy cuts in, "This was hardly more than ten minutes ago. They tased my husband, drugged him with some kind of rag soaked in something, and took our daughter Annie. She's eleven years old. They said if we call the police they'll kill her. They told me they would contact us tonight at our hotel with further instructions. Oh, God, they said if we talk to the police she's-"

"Just wait a minute." The officer holds a hand in the air and closes his eyes. He frowns for a moment, keeping his eyes closed as if he's deep in thought, pondering something intensely. Then, opening his eyes, he says slowly, "Start from the beginning."

We tell him everything, starting from the moment we met the man in the lobby of our hotel.

And as Judy and I retell the story, with each passing second I feel my heart sinking further and further into my stomach.

They're going to kill her, aren't they? And we didn't even *go* to the police. We *tried* to follow their orders. We weren't going to the police.

But what does it matter at this point? It's a lost cause.

Because the police came to *us*.

Chapter Six
Annie

"Be quiet and everything will be okay. Hey, do you hear me?" The tour guide stares at me angrily as the man driving the van drives fast down the bumpy road. I don't know where they are taking me. I'm curled up in the back of the van. I tried grabbing the door handle, but it's locked. The tour guide sits in the back seat and glares back at me.

"Hey, if you don't be quiet, your mom and dad will get hurt. How does that sound to you? You don't want us to hurt them, do you?" The tour guide's lip twitches.

Somehow, I manage to stop crying. I wipe my eyes and turn my head to look at the man who I thought was just a normal tour guide. Isn't that what Dad said? But this doesn't seem like part of the tour. Something is wrong. Why did they take me and leave Mom and Dad? And I think he hurt Dad – that's what it looked like to me, it looked like he hit him with something before that other man, the driver, put me in the back of this van. I'm so scared right now, but I'm trying not to be. Mom always taught me to be strong. So did Dad. They always told me to face my fears and be brave.

But I don't think they were ever talking about something like this.

"Hey, listen. Everything is going to be okay. This is just a game we're playing with your parents."

"A game? What game?" I sniffle.

"They're gonna give us a reward for giving you back. That's the game!" He grins. "Simple, huh?"

"I don't understand," I say.

"Hey, don't sweat it. It's just a game, like I said. Nothin' serious. I'm just a tour guide, okay? This is… This is kind of part of the tour, okay? You're going to see your folks in no time – under one condition – you stay quiet and stay out of our way, and don't try to escape. You try to escape, well… That's just about the worst thing you could try to do. And believe me, you won't get very far. Maybe about five feet – and that'll be the last five feet you ever walk on your own two legs. I don't like saying mean things like that, but I'm not going to lie to you. And don't even get me started on what'll happen to your parents if you try to escape… We won't be very nice to them, will we?" He looks up at the driver, who grunts something and shakes his head, keeping his eyes intently on the road.

"Where are you taking me?" I ask.

The tour guide seems to have grown tired of talking. He waves his hand and says, "Don't worry about it. I think I explained everything pretty clearly to you, so now all you gotta do is sit back, relax, and wait for your folks to pony up the money. Okay?"

His lips draw up past his teeth as he grins at me, but there is nothing friendly about his smile.

Chapter Seven
Judy

The two police officers stare at us with dumbfounded expressions. Clearly they weren't expecting this when they responded to a call about screaming. They thought it was going to be a simple, routine domestic violence call, I suppose.

They run us through a string of questions as I shout back at them and demand to speak to someone higher up. At this point, we've already gotten ourselves into a potentially horrific outcome by talking to the police, but there was no other choice. It's not like we sought them out. They just showed up, and we had the choice to either get arrested or explain the situation.

And believe me, I'm trying my hardest to stay calm while explaining the situation to these men, but it's the most difficult thing I've ever done, because my daughter is out there and I don't know what is going to happen to her.

"Okay, okay. You two are upset. I understand that. If what you are telling us is true, then you've got every right to be upset. Look, here's what we're going to do. We're going to take the two of you downtown and you're going to tell this same story to Detective Elrod. Okay?"

My head throbs as my mind races a million miles a minute. I feel completely hopeless, trapped, and I have no clue what to do. Bruce and I have found ourselves in the worst possible situation either of us could ever imagine. Despite our differences as husband and wife, we are both crazy about our daughter and would die for her. And now here we both are, standing in front of two police officers when the kidnapper warned us just minutes ago not to go to the police.

I pray he was bluffing. He made it sound like he would somehow know. But how? That would be too elaborate of a conspiracy. It was just two men who took her, and now they are gone. Long gone. To where, I don't know.

Where is my daughter?

The next twenty or thirty minutes are a blur. I guess we get into the back seat of the police car because I remember seeing city lights flashing by and hearing sirens and car horns and seeing the dirty, snow-covered city streets pass us by. Then a moment later we seem to be sitting in an interrogation room. The two officers are standing at either side of a square-jawed sixty-something year old man with a thick head of curly gray hair and a stern set of icy blue eyes. He gazes at us with his cold eyes and pursed lips, nodding his head occasionally. Sometimes he makes a curious expression by tilting his head to the side and furrowing his brow as we tell the story again. But mostly he just looks tired.

"Please," I plead. "We're running out of time, and I know we're already in hot water by coming here and talking to you – but it's not like we had a choice."

He nods his head slowly and slides the tip of his tongue across his lower lip, staring down at the table as he sighs. "In a minute we'll get a sketch artist in here and I'll have you two give as detailed a description as possible. Okay? That should help; having his face out there to be looked for." He turns and glares at the two officers and then jerks a thumb at them. They quickly hurry from the room, leaving us alone with Detective Elrod, who says nothing else. He just sits there twisting a pen around in his fingers, staring down at his desk. I can't tell if he is grumpy, bored, or deep in thought about the case.

A moment later the two officers return with another man, this one dressed in plain clothes - perhaps he is not a police officer. But I don't know. I don't know anything right now and in all honesty I feel more clueless than I've ever felt.

"This man is going to draw up a sketch of the suspect, so please describe him in great detail," Detective Elrod says.

I go over the description again along with Bruce. My headache has gotten worse – it's stress, no doubt. I have no idea what is going to happen next and the feeling of not knowing makes everything so much worse.

After all is said and done, the sketch artist holds up a startlingly accurate looking sketch of the man who drove us to the parking structure. I nod my head, feeling an icy chill running down my spine as I stare at the sketch. The black and white drawing seems to morph into his actual face, pale and freckled with light, wispy hair. I see him staring at me, laughing, his thin cheekbones jutting out as his smile fills the room.

"Ma'am." Detective Elrod has his hand on my shoulder.

I feel like I've just woken up from a dream. Bruce is sitting next to me, giving me a worried look. His cheeks have a pale, sickly color to them, and his eyes are bloodshot.

"Honey?"

"I'm okay," I say. "I just remembered him once I saw the sketch. It looks just like him," I murmur.

Bruce reaches over and wraps his arms around me awkwardly from the chair next to mine. Then he pulls away and his body seems to curl up into itself, shrinking. He shouts suddenly, twisting his head towards the detective and officers. "They want a million dollars? God, if I had that, I'd pay it in a heartbeat. Money means nothing to me right now. But the problem is I don't have *close* to that. My business has been failing for the last two years now and I'm on my way to bankruptcy if I don't turn it around. I play the part of a wealthy businessman, but I've got probably a quarter of a million and I can't simply go to the ATM and withdraw that – and if I could, so what? They don't want a *quarter* of a million. They want a million or she's dead. They're going to *kill* her if I don't pay them an amount I don't have." His voice ricochets. He stands up suddenly and begins pacing the room, his red face dripping sweat. "I've got to get out of here. We've got to get to the hotel. They're going to call us later there. But what does it matter? I don't have the money they want."

"Oh, God, Bruce." My stomach rises up into my throat, and I close my eyes and try to focus on breathing.

He turns to me, eyes bulging, lips shaking, and tosses his hands in the air. "You've got a separate business bank account. I'm guessing you don't have enough to make it even close to a million, do you?" He licks his lips nervously. He knows the answer, of course.

I shake my head. I've got a decent amount saved, but nothing close to what we need to get Annie back. I never realized it until now – I thought we had so much more money in our joint bank account, but I simply never bothered to check, or at least I haven't bothered to check in the last couple years.

"I'm going to need you to get me the information on this tour company," Detective Elrod says.

Bruce fumbles with his phone and seems to pull up the email. He shows it to Elrod, who takes the phone and thumbs through it, then stands up and leaves the room. Some time passes, maybe fifteen or twenty minutes, and then he walks back into the room and sighs. He hands Bruce the phone.

"Company's legit, but there's no answer. Something's fishy, and I don't know what."

"What does that mean?" I say.

"It means a tour guide with a website that big and close to a thousand seemingly legitimate reviews wouldn't ignore a phone call from a potential customer. Something is off. We've got men looking into it now. They're going to check out the address of the headquarters. It's supposedly in Red Hook."

"Well, where's that?" Bruce asks wearily.

"It's in Brooklyn."

Bruce, with his elbows propped up on his knees and his hands rubbing his tired face, stares down at the ground and says, "What do we do now?"

"Now we wait."

Detective Elrod checks his watch and leans back in his seat, staring at us as he crosses his arms. I can't read him. I don't know what he's thinking or what he's planning, but I feel like death right now as I sit here shaking, wondering what's happening to my sweet Annie.

Panic bores down on me, taking over every inch of my mind and body. What are we going to do? How are we going to get her back?

It's okay, I tell myself. *Deep breaths. You'll get her back. You will – don't worry.*

I tell myself we're going to figure this out. I tell myself we're going to settle this one way or another and get our daughter back safely. I tell myself that soon I'll be holding her in my arms and feeling her skin against mine, feeling her breath and hearing her laughter.

But I know that isn't true. Because we don't have the ransom money they're demanding.

And if we don't have the ransom money, then our daughter is as good as dead.

An hour passes. It is the longest hour of my life. Then Elrod's cell phone rings. He picks it up and speaks casually into the line. "Tell me."

A moment later his brow furrows into a dozen big, deep set wrinkles as he stares off past us, mouth slightly ajar. "Maitland was the one who registered the business. He was the owner." He sighs into the phone, leaning forward in his seat with his elbow propped up on the desk. "Well, okay. Keep me posted."

He puts his phone back in his pocket and moves his eyes to us once again. Then he takes a breath and sucks anxiously on his lips as he says, "This company was owned by a man named George Maitland. We ran the plates and the car in the garage belongs to him. That was George Maitland's car you were riding in, but Maitland wasn't driving it. He was just found dead in his office. Been dead at least a day or so. He was shot point blank in the head three times."

"Oh my God," Bruce murmurs, clutching my arm as he leans forward.

"So far we're aware of two other full time employees Maitland had on the payroll. Based on the schedule he had on his desk, they were both scheduled to be giving tours in separate parts of the city today. One of them is all the way out in Coney Island. Maitland himself, it seems, was scheduled to give your family a tour. So he's not *just* the owner; he also works as a guide himself. It doesn't sound like this driver you had was truly employed there, whoever he is – Tony, or whatever his real name may be - but I don't know. Too bad you say he was wearing driving gloves, otherwise his prints would be all over the vehicle. A guy like this surely has a criminal record. This ain't his first rodeo. My men are sorting through employment records, so we'll know for certain soon. All I know is that this is obviously not a coincidence. Whoever shot Maitland has got to be the same person who kidnapped your daughter. Doesn't take a rocket scientist to figure that out. Not necessarily this Tony fellow – it could be the other one you said was with him." He pauses, squinting down at the table before looking back up at us. "You're sure you didn't get any sort of look at the other guy's face?"

"No," I say softly as my heart thuds relentlessly. "It happened so fast, and he was mostly in the shadows. I think the only thing I noticed about him was his shaggy brown hair."

"Shaggy brown hair," Elrod repeats, twirling his pen between his fingers. He stares up at us and sighs. "I know you folks are going through hell right now to say the very least, but I want you to know that we're going to find your daughter. We might even find her before this handoff of the money is supposed to take place, whenever that may be. We'll see what the kidnappers say on the phone tonight. But don't worry. We'll get her back."

I try to believe the detective, I really do, but I can't seem to feel anything but hopelessness. I don't know how I'm going to get through these next two days without losing my mind.

Chapter Eight
Judy

At six fifteen the phone rings in the living room of our hotel suite. I reach for it shakily and put it to my ear. I have been instructed on what to say. Four technicians sit between Bruce and me, along with Detective Elrod and several other police officers. Everyone looks on edge, Bruce most of all.

"Hello," I say softly.

"You'll have the million ready?" A cold voice greets me on the other line.

"Yes. We've arranged to receive the money from our bank the day after tomorrow." I say, staring up at Detective Elrod. This is a lie.

"Good. Then in two days, on the evening of the fourth, you are to stand with your husband on West 105th and Columbus at eight thirty p.m. next to the crosswalk in front of Vincenzo's Deli. You will not be with anyone else or your daughter dies. If we think the police are planted nearby, your daughter dies. You will be carrying a suitcase with the money in it. And one other thing – if the bills are marked, the deal is off, and your daughter dies. No tricks."

"Will you have her with you? After we hand over the suitcase, you'll give her back, right?"

"Yes, if there are no tricks. A million dollars in cash. Unmarked bills. No exceptions. Do not try to play games with us."

"I understand. So you'll count it and then hand her over?" My voice shakes desperately.

"No tricks." He says again, and then the line goes dead.

Detective Elrod moves his eyes swiftly down to the technicians.

"He ended it too soon. We almost had a location," one of them says.

Elrod curses angrily and punches the air. Then he gives Bruce and me a hard stare. "You'll do what he says. You'll stand there with the suitcase. It'll have a million dollars in it, but he won't get a chance to even begin counting it before we nab him. We don't pay ransoms in this country. But we can pretend to." He pauses, smirking. "So they'll pick it up at 105th and Columbus and then we'll nab 'em hard and fast before they get a chance to even know what hit 'em."

"How? He said if there are police nearby-"

"To *hell* with what he said. He won't know any police are nearby, but I'll have them posted on every corner. That little weasel turns right; they'll nab him before he drives ten feet. He turns left, same story. He goes straight; I'll have four officers parked on either side of the road in civilian cars ready to swerve in front of his, blocking it from moving an inch. Hell, I'll have them crash right into his car if I have to," he shouts. "They'll get out waving their guns and be on top of those sniveling little worms in two seconds flat. It'll be the last thing this 'Tony' clown ever expects to happen. I've been doing this a long time, and I've always been successful in organizing sting operations. I could plant a hundred of my men on a three block radius and no one would bat an eye or think they were cops. I'm good at this." Little beads of sweat drip down his flushed cheeks as he stares at me with bulging eyes. He straightens his tie and cracks his head from side to side.

I turn to look at Bruce, feeling disoriented. Two days. Two days of agony, not knowing what is happening with our daughter. Two days until we can *possibly* finish this. Possibly. And what if we're making a big mistake? We don't have a million dollars to give them. What if this plan the detective is organizing doesn't pan out the way he wants it to?

What if the kidnappers know we're tricking them?

We're supposed to be carrying a suitcase stuffed with a million dollars, and then what? The cops will rush in and arrest the driver? Will it be Tony, the fake tour guide, or does he have someone working for him as a pick-up guy? Will it be the other guy, or is there possibly a third man we don't even know about? If it's someone working for Tony, what happens then? What if the pick-up guy doesn't contact Tony to let him know he got the money?

What then? Will Tony kill Annie?

My mind races with a million different scenarios, all of them bad, and I feel a queasiness rising up from the depths of my empty stomach. I haven't eaten anything today, but the thought of food makes me feel even more ill. I know I will be in physical and mental shambles until we get Annie back.

If we get her back.

No, don't think that way, I tell myself. *You're going to get her back.*

You will.

Although I tell myself this, I don't know if I believe it. Am I simply telling myself what I *want* to believe? They've got our daughter, and I'm feeling myself slipping mentally – I'm not sure how much longer I'm going to be able to keep myself together before I break down in tears and turn into a blubbering mess.

Who am I kidding? I've already turned into that. My eyes haven't been dry for a minute since it happened.

But I can't let myself succumb to the anxiety I'm feeling. If I do that, then there will be no hope left at all.

I've got to stay strong. Somehow, I've got to.

Chapter Nine
Annie

The cold, wet room smells the way I remember my grandmother's basement smelling, except this is much worse and much stronger.

I don't know where they took me. They put something over my eyes for about a minute when they led me from the back of the van into the room I'm in now. I've hardly seen them since that happened, except a few times when they brought me food and snacks. I'm not hungry because I'm so nervous, but I know I have to eat because if I don't I will get sick feeling. That's what Mom always told me when I tried skipping breakfast during fifth grade. She would always have me eat oatmeal in the morning or eggs and bacon.

I stare at the plate of food on the floor across from me. They left it there about an hour ago, but I haven't touched it. It's a sandwich and some French fries. I feel like crying as I stare at it because it reminds me of Mom telling me I better eat. As I shuffle over to the plate and grab the sandwich and put it to my lips, I feel like I can hear her voice saying: *"Now, sweetie, if you don't eat your breakfast you'll be feeling pretty bad in no time. You don't want a headache, do you?"*

I wish she were here now to tell me that. Instead I'm all alone in this dark, wet room. It's so creepy in here and so quiet. Sometimes I hear dogs barking outside. They sound wild. Other than that, I don't hear anything except cars driving by sometimes. I can't see out the window because the glass is so old and dirty from the outside. I feel like I'm in some old, abandoned warehouse. And I don't mean abandoned a few weeks ago. This place feels like it's been empty for years. The little room I'm in doesn't have anything in it except some old, empty shelves and a door which is locked of course. I tried to open it, but I couldn't.

I don't know how much time has passed. Has it been a day yet? A few hours? Has it been a week? I fell asleep for a while and I was dreaming, and now I don't know what's a dream and what's real. I hope I'm just dreaming now. I hope that any minute I'll wake up and see Mom nudging me to get up for school. Maybe this whole vacation was just a dream and I'm in my bed in San Francisco and it's six forty five in the morning and Mom is about to call my name and tell me it's time to get ready for school.

A rat runs quickly across the floor a few feet from where I lay and it makes me jump up and stumble up against the wall. I stand there with my back against it as I watch the rat disappear into a small hole in the floorboards. I wish I was as small as that little rat. I'd be able to get out of here in no time. I'd just slip out without being noticed and find my way across the city to wherever our hotel is. I'd find my parents and hug them tight and tell them I loved them and that I was sorry for ever doing anything bad.

I shiver as I realize this is not a dream.

This is real, and there is nothing I can do about it. No matter how much Mom and Dad taught me not to be scared of the boogeyman under my bed, it didn't help to prepare me for something like this, because this is real, and it's so much worse than my childhood fears of a man in my closet or a monster under my bed.

Suddenly, the door opens, and I see him standing there leaned up against the doorway – the man who was our tour guide, the one who picked us up at the hotel and pretended to be so normal and kind. He stares at me with one eyebrow raised higher than the other, then he looks away from me. His eyes move all around the room before focusing once more on me.

"What was that noise?" He asks. "Were you trying to escape? I warned you about trying to escape. Don't you remember what I said? About what would happen to your parents?"

"I wasn't trying to escape."

"What was that noise then?"

"I saw a rat. It scared me. I jumped."

"A rat." He grins and pulls a cigarette from his shirt pocket, tosses it between his lips, and lights it. He takes a long puff of it and blows the smoke into the small room where I stand up against the wall in the corner. It smells terrible. He chuckles and says again, "A rat." After sucking some more smoke into his mouth he says in a cold voice, "Next time you see a rat, don't make me think you're trying to break through the wall. Bad things will happen to your folks if I think that. You understand what I'm telling you?"

"Yes," I say.

"Good," he says, and slams the door shut, leaving me all alone again – just me and the rat, who I see poking his little head up from the hole in the floorboards. He's not so bad after all, I guess. In a way, he's kind of cute. If I stay in here long enough, maybe he'll become my one and only friend.

I start crying, but I try to do it quietly.

I don't want the mean man to hear me. If he does, he might get annoyed and hurt me or my mom and dad. I don't know what I'm going to do, but I hope somebody rescues me, because I know there's no way I can rescue myself.

Mom taught me the word 'hopeless' when I was a little kid. I remember thinking it sounded cool when I heard someone say it in a movie for some reason, but she told me the meaning of the word wasn't cool at all and was actually pretty sad. She said it wasn't a happy word.

I guess that the word hopeless is a good way to describe how I am feeling right now. I feel like there is no way out of this situation I'm in. I wonder what Mom and Dad are thinking right now. I hope they miss me as much as I miss them. I'm sure they do. I'm lucky I have such nice parents. I wish I had told them that before the mean man took me away. I hope I will get a chance to tell them that sometime.

I hope I'm not going to be stuck in this empty, stinky, wet room forever.

Chapter Ten
Bruce

The next two days move at a snail's pace and are without question the darkest days of my life.

But what if things get even darker?

I try not to think that way. I try to envision seeing Annie again, seeing her smiling face looking at me as sunlight beams behind her golden hair. I try to tell myself that we're going to get our daughter back, but with each passing hour and the lack of updates from Detective Elrod, I begin to lose hope.

I spend most of the time in the hotel room with Judy. It's not as if we've gone out sightseeing. We're both stuck here on the verge of being unable to function. Neither of us have been able to eat for the last two days, save for small bites of sandwiches or plain white bread here and there. Any more than that and we both begin to feel as if we are going to be sick. A police officer has been staying with us in the event that the phone rings again, but we haven't heard a thing, and I don't expect to. Other than sitting in the room, I've taken lots of walks down the hallway of the hotel – back and forth, walking aimlessly along the halls of the forty-second floor like a zombie.

It's drawing nearer to the pickup time. We've got two hours to go. The doorbell rings and the officer opens it. Detective Elrod comes in and wipes his shoes on the mat, then steps into the living room of the suite and surveys us. It's the first time we've seen him in about a day. He looks grave, which doesn't instill any confidence in me.

"You two ready for tonight?"

"Yes," I say.

"We've put up a safehouse on the third floor of a walkup on 106th and Columbus. It's got windows facing the avenue and my men will be able to see everything. Now, you two are going to take a cab to the location separately. From here on out until the handoff, you're on your own. This is, of course, to protect your daughter. We don't want these men thinking anything seems fishy, okay?"

"Okay," I say. Judy nods beside me. I clutch her by the arm and glance at her.

"There's a cab waiting for you downstairs outside the lobby. The driver works with us sometimes. His name is Enrique. He'll take you there." He hands over a suitcase. "Take this. It's got the money in it. Don't lose it, we'll need it back. And do me a favor, will ya? *Breathe.* You both look like you're on the verge of having a stroke. Two guys as stupid as this, trying to pull off a ransom in America in this day and age... They're not going to get away with it. But we're going to let them think they are. Rest assured, we've got this covered. All you've got to do is stand there on 105th and Columbus and hand over the suitcase when the driver pulls up."

I nod my head and try to breathe.

Ten minutes later we are in a cab heading north on Broadway. We swerve carefully around

Columbus Circle and then make our way up Central Park West heading uptown. Enrique drives silently, staring at the white road ahead of us. This afternoon it snowed again, and traffic moves slowly. I check my watch and see that we've still got plenty of time. In fact, I suspect we'll likely be standing there fifteen or twenty minutes early, just to be sure we don't miss them. I wouldn't be able to live with myself if we missed the handoff time.

What would happen if we didn't get there in time?

Judy stares out the window wordlessly, occasionally turning and staring in my direction. It pains me to see the worried expression on her face, and I pray that this is all over quickly. I hope with every fiber of my being that our daughter will be given back to us once the police have apprehended these awful men.

But my mind races with all sorts of terrible possibilities.

For instance, where will Annie be at the time of the handoff? The back seat? Or, God forbid, what if they're lying? What if we hand over the money and Annie isn't even in the car with them? If not, then will they have her at an undisclosed location being watched by someone? Who will that someone be? Will they be waiting for an order from Tony, or whoever the pickup guy is? Will they be waiting for a signal?

And, of course, the terrifying thought I had earlier comes back to me – the thought that if the police apprehend the driver, then the person watching Annie will kill her.

I hope desperately that she is in the car like they said she would be, because if she is not, then this plan Detective Elrod has come up with seems awfully flimsy.

Counting a million dollars takes time, and they can't simply do that on a New York street corner while double-parked on the edge of the road, can they?

I don't know. I don't know anything about the neighborhood we're going to, and it makes me sick to think about how clueless I am. I feel powerless right now, at the mercy of vicious, lowlife criminals, and I don't know how to escape this feeling. I just know that I have to get Annie back. If I don't, then I'll never be able to function again. If they kill her, then they might as well kill me, because I'll go mad.

"We're here," Enrique says. I turn and stare out the door window. We are on 104th and Columbus. Enrique points up ahead. "Right up there on the next block is 105th. There's the deli you're supposed to stand in front of. Elrod said stand at the edge of the road, right by the crosswalk. Good luck." He gives us a sympathetic looking grin.

I stare at Judy, she stares back at me, and then we both get out of the cab, me holding the suitcase, and stumble through the snow towards the next block. My heart feels like it's bouncing around my throat. I have never felt such tremendous anxiety in all my life, and as I check my watch I see that my hand is shaking. We have ten minutes to go.

We reach 105th and Columbus Avenue and we stand there by the crosswalk staring back and forth along the road. I check my watch incessantly as I scan our surroundings. It isn't Times Square by any means, or anywhere even close it in terms of foot traffic, but about six people have passed us in the last minute going about their business, so this isn't an isolated spot. I wonder what made him pick this block? Do they live around here? Do they have some spot where they're keeping our daughter around here? Was it a random location on the map he pointed at?

My heart beats like a drum. Eight twenty eight. My brain feels as if it is gyrating in my skull. I stare down the boulevard, watching as cars roll southbound down the one way avenue. I check my watch. Eight twenty nine.

At exactly eight thirty, a black sedan pulls up to the curb just in front of where we stand at the edge of the street. A back door opens and a man with shaggy brown hair appears in the dark interior of the vehicle.

"Get in the car," he says.

"What?" I murmur.

"Get in the car or we'll kill her right now." He hisses angrily.

Moving with the instincts of a dancer, I quickly take a step and drop down into the back seat as the man moves over to give me room. Judy follows me.

"Where is our daughter?" I say.

"Shut up. I'll ask the questions and you'll respond. If you don't respond then your daughter won't be breathing much longer." His expression is stern and confident. He stares at me without blinking and then caresses the suitcase. "I assume if I open this up and count it then there will be a million dollars in unmarked bills, am I correct?"

"Yes."

"Good. Well, there's not much time to do that here, so we'll take you somewhere and count the money there." He glances up at the driver. It's then that I realize I've been too stunned to even look up in that direction since sitting down in the back seat. The driver is Tony, if that's his real name, and he stares back at me like we've never even met. His blank face looks like the face of a psychopath, until a sudden glimmer comes over his eyes and a smile curls up at the corners of his lips. His eyes shift over to the passenger seat. It's then that I see Annie sitting there silently.

Tony chuckles. "I told her to not cause any trouble or else I'd hurt Mommy and Daddy. Isn't that right, Annie? Isn't that what your friend Tony told you?" He looks at her and grins.

Annie says nothing. She doesn't even look back at me, but I can see she's trembling slightly.

I want to *kill* these men with my bare hands.

"Don't worry," he continues, his eyes back on me again. A smirk fills his face that I'd like to wipe off. "We didn't hurt your daughter. She didn't cause us any trouble. But we won't hesitate to – if you've tried to trick us." He looks at the man with shaggy hair sitting beside me. "Blindfolds?"

"What?" I murmur.

What are the cops waiting for? What on earth is happening?

I guess they didn't account for the possibility of us getting into the vehicle. I didn't account for that possibility either.

Stupid, stupid! What were we thinking? Everyone seemed to expect it to be a simple handoff. Maybe they'd spend a few minutes counting the money, then they'd hand her over. Then the cops would show up and save the day.

It isn't happening like that at all, is it?

"Blindfolds?" I say.

"For the ride. Then we'll count the money, leave the three of you there safe and unharmed, and five minutes after you hear the last of our footsteps, you'll be able to remove the blindfolds and go back to your life."

Before either of us can say anything, the man slides a blindfold over each of our faces. Then the car begins to move; I feel it turning right. A moment later I hear a sudden gasp from inside the vehicle, followed by screams from outside on the street. Screams from police.

"Stop the car! Stop or I'll shoot!"

I hear Tony slamming his foot loudly on the gas pedal and then the car jolts forward after burning rubber. "They double crossed us! They double crossed us, man!" A voice shouts. I reach for the blindfold but feel someone hit the side of my face.

"*Don't move! You set us up, and now you're going to pay.*" The voice slithers.

This is our only chance. I can't sit here blindfolded and die in the dark, knowing my wife and daughter are going to suffer the same fate.

I have to fight.

I start flailing my fists blindly, feeling them colliding with the man to my right. Then I feel Judy moving behind me. I rip the blindfold from my head and twist around to see her reaching up and grabbing Tony by the throat as she screeches. The car swerves on the narrow road, weaving all around as Tony lets out a guttural sounding gasp and then begins gagging. The man at my side, with his nose bloodied from my fist, is reaching down for his gun. He must have dropped it on the floorboard during all the commotion.

Snarling, I grab him by the throat and slam him up against the window. We look into each other's eyes, both of us growling with rage and fear as we fight for our lives like wild animals. It is a dark, primal feeling I have never felt before. The man's face is ripe with panic as his eyes shift from me down to the floorboard where the gun lies waiting to be used. He is still reaching for it as I hold onto him, frantically trying to grab ahold of it as he howls; spit flying from his mouth.

Judy's screams grow louder. The car swerves more violently.

Then I feel something slam into us from behind, and that's when the car loses control altogether, flying up onto the sidewalk and slamming into a brownstone. Then everything goes dark for a minute.

Chapter Eleven
Judy

"It's over, Judy. It's all over."

Bruce is beside me. His face is battered and blood drips from his nose. We're standing outside the car. This has all felt like a horrible dream.

"Where's Annie?" I whisper.

"She's right here," Bruce says.

My panic immediately dissipates when I see our sweet daughter standing beside Bruce. She looks shaken, but that doesn't stop her from rushing over and wrapping her arms around me. I hold her closely, crying uncontrollably as I feel her body heat radiating against mine. I have never felt so grateful for anything in my life, and I know that I never will. Despite trying to remain hopeful, deep down I feared for the worst, and part of me felt like this was the end for all of us – if Annie was dead, I know that Bruce and I would be completely broken.

But she isn't. She's right here hugging me, with Bruce standing beside us, crying almost as hard as I am. A surge of emotions bores through me like a rollercoaster as I try to comprehend how we got to this point.

I remember everything, but the crash happened so suddenly, and then things got fuzzy for me. I didn't black out, but it all happened so quickly that I just couldn't take it in. I remember holding the driver by the throat, watching him struggling to breathe, and then feeling the car crash into us from behind. That must have been the police. After that I remember him swerving off the road. The next thing I knew, I was standing there with Bruce at my side.

It's over. It's over.

It's really over.

Paramedics come and check us out, demanding we go to the hospital to be checked for injuries. All I want to do is hold my daughter. I agree to go to the hospital to be taken for scans but only under the condition that I'm with Annie the whole time. I feel so worried now, so horribly stressed about how she was taken from us out of the blue. Our world was turned upside down in a matter of seconds, and I can't let that happen again.

But I shouldn't worry, because that was a freak incident, and it's over now. They got the men who did this. Both of them.

A day passes and it feels like an hour. Our scans are clear and we're all without injuries from the crash. We're all just a bit dehydrated, but we're able to get that under control. We are seated in a room at the police station, just the three of us as we wait. Annie has been surprisingly resilient this entire time. I think that she is going to bounce back in no time, although I know she may need lots of help in doing so. She says that neither of the men hurt her, but they threatened to and told her that they would hurt us if she tried to escape.

Detective Elrod walks into the room and drops a file on the table. With him is a brunette with a friendly smile. "We've got someone here who would like to talk to Annie. She's a specialist who deals with these things – traumatic events for kids. Annie, this is Mrs. Miles. Mrs. Miles would like to talk to you for a few minutes."

"Okay." Annie nods.

They go out of the room together. I'm reluctant to watch her go, but I know she'll be fine. When the door closes, I feel my head drop down and I take a long, shaky breath.

"We've got a whole lot of information now about the two men who took her." Elrod sits down across from us and pauses. "Or the man and the boy, I should say. They're brothers, and the one named Tony is a minor. Believe it or not, that's his real name. He didn't even think to use an alias. Sixteen years old and still in high school. Or was. I'm not supposed to talk about the details now since it's an ongoing investigation involving a minor, even with you being involved in the case, but I don't mind bending the rules a bit right now because I know you were put through the ringer and you deserve some information."

"I should have known. We asked him how old he was because he looked so young. He told us nineteen." Bruce stares at me before turning back to Detective Elrod. "So, what happens now?" He sighs.

"His brother is twenty-five. Neither of them have much of a home life. They came from a rotten family. His brother doesn't seem to have a lot of remorse for what he did, though. His name's

Freddy." Elrod pauses, rubbing his eyes. "*Tony*, on the other hand, well... Let's just say I've never seen so much bawling in all my career as an officer. The kid's been in a non-stop crying fit ever since we brought him in. Answered all our questions, told us everything we needed to know and even volunteered more information that we *didn't* need to know. Says his brother bullied him and made him do it, threatening him, and threatening to hurt their mother, apparently, even though their mother is pretty much out of the picture and lives in New Jersey. They live with an aunt in New York. It's a sad situation, really. This Tony kid really thought his brother Freddy was going to hurt their mom. He still cares about her despite her abandoning them both – or that's what he says, at least."

"So, I'm guessing he's going to get off with a smack on the wrists?" I say, biting my lip.

"No, I wouldn't say that. He committed a serious crime, despite him claiming to have been coerced into doing so by his older brother. His brother murdered a business owner, although Tony says he wasn't aware of that. But then together they kidnapped a child - *your* child. That's a serious offense for Tony, even if he wasn't involved in the murder. Anyway, Freddy seems to have scoped the place out after killing the man – the tour company, I mean - and he must've decided to try and pick some tourists who were very wealthy, and so they settled on you. Who knows why they didn't just pick a random family they saw living on 5th Avenue. Most young criminals aren't very smart. Sometimes their crimes don't make a whole lot of sense – and from what Tony tells us; his brother simply seemed to think it would be 'fun.' *Fun*, can you believe that? Makes me sick." Detective Elrod pauses, shaking his head.

He continues, "I won't lie to you folks, though – his age and his being potentially coerced into this is going to have a big effect on the outcome. I'd be surprised if Tony does a whole lot of time. He's a minor, and he's squeaky clean, other than this, but his brother isn't. Freddy's got a big rap sheet, and I suspect he'll go down for life."

"What if this kid's lying about it all?" Bruce says angrily. "What if he's just trying to garner sympathy? He was just as involved as his older brother. It doesn't matter if he's sixteen. He doesn't feel remorse. You should've seen his face – that sneer on his face."

"It matters to a judge, and it matters in the eyes of a jury," Elrod says, holding his arms up innocently. "But there's no way he gets off without doing time. He's going to serve time for this. You don't kidnap a kid and demand a ransom without serving time for it, even if your brother talked you into it. Even if you're a minor. But look, your daughter is safe. She's back in your arms. This whole thing could have gone so much worse."

"Yeah," Bruce says, sighing. He slumps over the table. "I'm just glad we got here. Oh, God, I feared the worst."

"So did I." Detective Elrod nods.

He's right. I don't like the idea of this Tony kid getting a short sentence for what he did, but he's right. We got her back. We got Annie back and everything is okay now. That's all that matters, and the older brother is going to go to prison for a long time. I'm sure of it.

Soon those two brothers will be a distant memory.

Chapter Twelve
Bruce

Seven Years Later

A dense fog rolls in from the sea as I sip my coffee and stare out through the windows of the café. It's twelve p.m. on a Wednesday in mid-June and I'm enjoying a much deserved break from work. I think after this I'll head over to Sal's and grab a turkey sandwich before heading back into the office. In the last six and a half years, things have improved majorly in terms of business.

Although it wasn't immediate. For about a year after the kidnapping, which is a memory we hardly ever speak of these days, my business continued going down. It wasn't until a colleague and I went into business together and came up with a good investment idea that things began to trend upward, and from then on things essentially skyrocketed. After that, I made some major changes in our lifestyle – not being wasteful by any means, but simply not being as tight about money as I was before. I took more vacations with Judy and Annie, making sure to take at least a month off from work each year and spend that month with my family.

Judy has certainly liked the change, and it brought us closer in the end. But what really seemed to bring us closer was the event that happened in New York that winter with Annie being taken. I don't know what I'd have done if things had gone differently, but I know I probably would have lost my mind at the very least. But Judy bounced back quickly and after a while that horrific ordeal was rarely mentioned again by any of us.

Now, Annie is eighteen and I can't believe the woman she's become. She graduated high school with wonderful grades, got accepted into UCLA, and starts in the fall. It's quite surreal to see how she has grown. She was always so bright, but now she's about to start her journey towards adulthood. Intelligence wise, she definitely takes after her mother – thank goodness. The thought makes me chuckle as I finish my coffee and stand up, stretch, and go out the front door into the gloomy San Francisco fog.

After a quick lunch at Sal's I head back to the office, not having very far to walk. I have a small space on the third floor of a building in the Financial District. It's quaint, but it's all the space I need. When I reach the front of the building and head through the front doors I hear someone calling my name from behind.

"Hey, Mr. Hurt? Bruce Hurt?" It is a voice I don't recognize, but I do business with all sorts of people, so I figure it's someone I've worked with before once or twice.

I turn and see a man standing with his hands in his coat pockets. He's about six feet tall, broad shouldered, with a thin face and a long neck. His hair is a sandy blonde and cut quite short. He smiles shyly at me before approaching and then sticks out a hand. "How you doing, Mr. Hurt?"

I'm reluctant to shake a stranger's hand, but I figure this is some young man I've met before – but where, and who is he? I stick my hand out and give him a flimsy shake. His hand is clammy, and he holds mine tight and squeezes it without letting go. As he does this he stares at me without blinking. The smile stays fixed on his thin face.

It's then that I feel a sudden chill passing through me and a startling sense of recognition. But no, it can't be – he went to prison. And that was all the way on the East Coast. It's just someone else whose face vaguely resembles his.

"You remember me now? I've grown a few inches and gotten a little wider." He keeps shaking my hand. He is squeezing it.

"Sorry, I can't say I do." I manage to pull my hand from his vice like grip. The bones feel sore from him squeezing so hard.

"I'm really sorry to bother you like this, but you giving me a moment of your time will mean the world to me. Almost seven years ago, Mr. Hurt. I did something very bad to your family in New York. I'm sure you saw the sentencing – I was given close to seven years since I was a minor, but my brother got life since he was an adult and the one who planned it. Well, that, of course, but more because the fact that he shot that poor tour company owner. I didn't have anything to do with that part, Mr. Hurt – if you followed the court case you'd know that. I didn't know my brother shot anybody. He did that himself without me knowing before he put me up to the idea of pretending to be a tour guide, and all... He forced me into it, pretty much. So, I guess that's why the judge and the jury gave him a much harsher sentence, what with murder being involved and all..." He pauses for a moment, smiling. His smile is unnerving because it looks genuine, not angry.

Why is he smiling while telling me this?

He continues, "My brother got killed a couple years ago, though. Big fight in the yard. Got shanked. A shank is a homemade little knife, Mr. Hurt. Anyway, I wanted to make amends with you for what I did. I changed a lot in prison, became acquainted with the power of the Lord, and I wanted to let you know that I truly am sorry for what I did, and I ask for your forgiveness, and the forgiveness of your wife and daughter. Her name was Annie, I remember. And your wife was Judy, I believe. I hope they're doing well. I thought of you all the time in prison, of the three of you. The Lord has forgiven me for what I have done, but I hope you will as well. You and your family." He pauses, keeping his eyes fixed on mine. "You look great, Mr. Hurt. You really do. You haven't aged a day. You must be keeping yourself in shape somehow, going to the gym. I went to the gym some too while I was locked up." He glances down at his bulging chest and then back up at me, still grinning.

I feel frozen with shock as I keep my eyes glued to the cretin standing in front of me. He is right – he's grown a tremendous amount, both in height and width, looking almost like a bodybuilder now. He waves a hand pleadingly and says in a gentle voice, "Please, Mr. Hurt. I see the way you're looking at me and it's making me worried. Give me a chance to apologize. All I ask is for the forgiveness of you and your family."

"Don't come around here anymore," I say sharply. "Don't ever come around my family, or else. Do you understand that?" I point at him, waving my finger angrily.

The smile stays on his face. "I'm simply asking for the forgiveness of you and your wife and daughter."

"Go back to New York. You shouldn't have come here. Just go back to New York and I'll forget about this instead of calling the police. And believe me, I will do exactly that if you dare come around my family. You'd better listen to me, you little punk. I put you in prison once and I'm not afraid to do it again, this time for stalking."

He stares at me without saying another word, but the smile remains on his face as I walk backwards in through the revolving doors and into the lobby of my building. Even as I glare at him, he continues to smile as if I just complimented him on his outfit.

Finally, after about half a minute, I muster up the courage to turn my back to him, and I stumble towards the elevator, feeling lightheaded and confused. What did he come here for?

A wonderful, routine day has turned upside down so quickly, and now I feel overcome with a surge of stressful memories. I knew I'd never forget entirely about those men and what they did, but I never thought I would see either of them again, and now the feeling I felt that day when my daughter was kidnapped has returned.

I ride the elevator to the third floor, sweating all the way up despite the air conditioner blasting. As I walk down the hallway and fumble in my pocket for the office keys, I feel dizzy and racked with all sorts of emotions. Why did this have to happen now? Why on earth did he come back? I admit, I'd followed the short trial and knew he had been sentenced to something like six and a half or seven years, but I hadn't been keeping track of the time, and I didn't realize his release date was coming up. And for the love of God, I didn't expect him to travel across the country to see me when he got out.

It's been about seven years, and now he's out. And now he's *here*.

I remember Judy and I sitting in that hotel room in New York, feeling my stomach twisted in knots, unable to eat, unable to drink, unable to *function* on any sort of meaningful level as we waited for the drop-off – as we waited to see if our daughter was still alive.

I remember walking the halls of the hotel during times when I felt like I couldn't sit still, wandering back and forth along the forty-second floor. I'd clench my fists and sometimes stop in the middle of the hallway and feel like screaming. Not knowing if our daughter was alive or dead was the worst, most nightmarish feeling we could ever have gone through.

I thought the pain from those memories would never resurface. I thought the depressing memories of being stuck between the four walls of that hotel would never bother me again. But now he's back, and with him he's brought a whole swarm of horrific memories.

Why is he here? What does he *want*?

I don't buy that nonsense he tried to sell me about finding God and wanting to ask me for forgiveness. And so what if he did find God? I wouldn't ever forgive him, not after what he did – and call me sick, but I didn't feel a touch of sympathy after hearing what he told me about the fate his brother suffered. Killed in prison? That's unfortunate for him, but oh well.

I won't lose any sleep over that after the hell he put us through – the hell he put my *daughter* through.

I hesitate at first to call the police due to the fact that the man claims to be here simply to apologize, and I don't want to make this a bigger ordeal than it is, but then I realize that not calling them would be foolish. I mean, what if he's planning on stalking me? Or worse, stalking Judy or Annie?

I put the phone to my ear after dialing Lieutenant Bill Morton. I've known him for a long time and he's a good man. He sounds perturbed by the news but reassures me that nothing will likely happen and if it does, he'll be on the rotten little creep in no time, well before he can do any harm to my family.

"Just keep me updated, will you? It's good you called. I can't really do anything since he probably is gone now – I mean, I doubt he's posted up outside your office still – but if you'd like, I'll have a car sent around to check the area."

"That'd be nice, Bill. I appreciate it."

"It's nothing. I'm sorry that happened. It must have brought back some bad memories, seeing his face again."

"It did, yeah, but at first it was hard to recognize him. He's big. Tell your men to look out for someone about six feet tall and built like a linebacker. Looks like he could play college football."

"I'll do that. And don't worry. You're in good hands here in San Francisco."

"Thanks, Bill. Let's go get drinks soon. It's been too long."

"Let's do it, but remember I'm sober now, buddy. You'll be the only one doing any serious drinking. I'm fine with sodas." He chuckles.

"Sounds good. Talk to you soon, pal. Thanks again."

"See you, Bruce."

I feel a little reassured in knowing that Bill is aware of the situation now. Well, I guess I shouldn't even call it a situation – it's nothing so far other than a shocking little encounter, and I suspect it'll stay that way. I'm pretty sure I ended any idea that little creep had about sticking around town. I told him off and I'm sure he knew I was serious about it. I don't think he'll mess with me any further, and I certainly don't think he'll mess with my wife and daughter.

Or am I just telling myself that in order to cope with the frightening possibility that he will?

I spend the rest of the workday distracted and unable to focus on the tasks that need accomplishing. Once four o'clock rolls around I decide to call it quits an hour early. I've got to get out of this stuffy office and into the fresh air. I think the twenty minute walk home will do me some good. I've got to try to clear my head, because my mind feels flooded with all sorts of panicked thoughts right now.

I considered texting Judy when it happened but decided not to. Still, I was tempted multiple times ever since getting back to the office, but I managed to refrain. I know I need to wait until we're both home and do it face to face. She's at her studio now and if I'm remembering right, she said she would be home late since she had a client coming in at seven. That means I won't be able to tell her until around eight thirty when she gets in. And it might be even later, because I don't want to bring it up with Annie there. Not yet, at least.

I'll wait until after dinner. I hope I don't act strange. I'm not a good actor and that means Judy can always tell if something is wrong – even little things, like if I stubbed my toe and tried to hide the fact that it hurt a little. She's so intuitive, and I know she'll probably be able to see that I'm deep in thought about something. But I shouldn't be because what's there to think about? The creep came back to supposedly apologize, and I told him to get lost.

So I bet he's going to listen to me and do that. He'll get out of town and leave me alone and not bother my family. Yeah – I'm worrying over nothing. I'm sure I won't even see him again. And I'm sure he won't try to contact Judy, or God forbid, *Annie*. Will he?

Come on, Bruce. You're working yourself up now. The doctors told you to watch your blood pressure, remember? You've been doing so well at managing your stress, and now you're letting some little punk rile you up...

Well, he's not so little anymore.

Regardless, I suspect I'm just worrying over nothing. Tony probably expected me to be gracious and forgiving, but instead I was stern about it when I told him to go back to New York and not bother us. Despite the annoying smile on his face, I'm sure he was listening to the words I was saying. He knew I meant business. He knew not to mess with me.

I hope he'll listen.

Chapter Thirteen
Annie

I thumb through the paperbacks as I walk down the musty aisle of the old used bookstore.

I love coming to this place. It sounds weird, maybe, but I like the smell of old books more than almost anything. I find it so soothing and relaxing. I've been this way as long as I can remember, I guess – a lover of used books. I remember when I was a little kid, Dad would take me to the bookstore. It wasn't a used bookstore, though. Still, I remember loving sitting there and looking at the covers of all the books. Sometimes I would pick one out that was a little too old for me. Those kinds of books didn't have pictures in them. Just words. Lots of words.

But I remember finding the words so interesting, and I liked that the books would all tell me different stories. When I would open one up I would just lie there in bed and get lost in another world. I'd be totally swept up in whatever I was reading and forget about my homework, dinner, and everything else. I guess I'm still that little girl, but my tastes have changed a bit, understandably.

Now I like science fiction, mystery, fantasy, and even horror. I don't really have a preference, and I go through periods where sometimes I don't read a book for a month or two, but I always end up missing it so much, and when I start reading again I can't help but binge books. I've got a small stack in the cart I'm holding right now. I think I picked enough to last me for the next month. I know once I get to college I won't have as much time to read, or at least I won't have as much time to read fiction, so I'm trying to get in as much as I can right now since I've got so much free time.

After paying at the register, I walk out of the shop holding a fairly heavy bag of books. It's a nice feeling, knowing I'm carrying a bag full of some new worlds I can escape into, even if they're only fictional worlds. Not that my real life is anything I want to actually escape from. I'm happy with where I'm at and I'm excited for the future, but I think it's important for me to turn off all the noise sometimes and lose myself in another world. For me, it's like a form of meditation.

Mom and Dad like that I read. They seem to approve of whatever I do, to be honest. Not that they'd let me do anything crazy. But I guess I've been an easy kid. I don't have any siblings to compare myself to, but I know Dad mentioned that he's so glad I wasn't a big partier, because he said he would've worried himself sick if I'd ever been out late partying. It's just not something I was into. I wasn't a loner in school, but I also was never the prom queen. Most of the time I liked being home reading or watching movies, or out at the arcade with Heather and Nancy, my two closest friends.

Most people I went to school with don't know what happened to me. I mean, it was on the news for a while when I was younger, but that was when I was in middle school, so most kids weren't told about it by their parents back then because they were too young, and by the time I entered high school I had mostly new classmates. Besides, it was old news at that point. Nobody really knows about that crazy situation I went through in New York, and I'm glad.

I haven't thought a whole lot about it over the last three or four years, but right after it happened, I won't lie, I thought about it a lot. It really affected me as a kid. I tried to hide the fact that it did, but I don't think I was fooling Mom or Dad. They had me in therapy. I went to talk to a lady once a week, sometimes twice a week. I know they paid a lot of money for that, but they said it was important, and I think it really helped.

Even though I don't think about it a lot, there are still moments where I simply think about it for a second or two – brief memories of those horrible days flashing before my eyes. But the memories don't bother me anymore. Not like they used to. They used to give me nightmares and sometimes make me cry, but now they simply pass through me without making me feel anything. I guess it's true what they say about time healing wounds, at least in some cases. I'm glad it was true in mine. I'd hate to still be having nightmares about those guys.

I guess the reason I'm thinking about it right now is because I'm old enough to know that the younger of the two is getting out at some point. A couple years ago I searched online about the case and found that he was quickly sentenced to about six and a half years after it happened. Mom and Dad hadn't told me anything about those details back then because I'd been far too young. But when I got older I was naturally curious.

    I didn't let myself search for any other details because I didn't want to get consumed by what I read, and I didn't want those frightening memories to come rushing back. I guess I just didn't want them to become any more vivid than they already were by researching about the man. But I couldn't seem to stop myself from wondering when he would be released. From what I remember, it would be sometime this year. I won't lie, I've been thinking about it quite a bit lately over these last few months, wondering if he's a free man by now or if he's still stuck in prison until later in the year. I don't know exactly about the other one, the one who was older, but I know he received a far longer sentence. I think it was life.

    The strange thing was, that man never really made an impression on me. He mostly stayed in the shadows. It was the younger one who talked to me and bossed me around. The other one just drove the car and seemed to be pretty quiet. As I walk along Fisherman's Wharf and look out at the water I feel chilled by the memory of those men.

    "Stop thinking about 'em, then," I tell myself, and nod my head.

    That's good advice, and I think I'd better take it. I went for quite a long time without letting those memories bother me, and just this year they've begun creeping back up in my mind. I can't let that happen. I won't allow it. I'm a strong person just like my parents are, and I'm not going to let memories get me down, because those memories don't mean a thing.

The only thing that matters is the fact that what happened seven years ago is finished. Nothing like that is going to happen again. I'm eighteen and I'll be going off to college soon. I can't let those memories start haunting me again, not now, not when I've got to focus on my studies. Not ever.

So *what* if he's getting out sometime this year? I'm not going to let that bother me.

It's not like I'm ever going to have to see him again.

Chapter Fourteen
Judy

Something is wrong with Bruce.

I can tell by the way he's playing with his food, swirling the fork around and raising it about halfway before slowly dropping it back down onto the plate. For whatever reason he has no appetite. I suppose it's something work related, but that would be unusual since everything with Bruce's business has seemed to be smooth sailing for the last several years, so maybe it's something else.

"What's the matter?" I ask.

He looks up at me and appears to be startled. Just like I knew he would, he waves it off with a smile. I chuckle and shake my head as I cut into my steak. "Come on, honey. You aren't fooling anyone."

"Yeah, Dad. You've hardly eaten a bite," Annie says.

He lets out a little laugh as he shakes his head. Bruce not eating signifies something is majorly wrong, because he usually eats more than Annie and I combined. He leans back in his seat, smiling nervously, still shaking his head. He sighs, "I didn't want to do this with Annie at the table. But you're eighteen now so I think it would be a disservice to you if I kept it secret." He stares at her.

"What?" Annie puts her fork down. "What are you talking about, Dad?"

"I..." He hesitates.

"Bruce, what is it?" I ask.

"Okay, okay," he waves his hands, sighing once more. "The kid from New York," he says uneasily, avoiding eye contact. "The driver. Tony. He showed up at my office today, out front on the street."

"What?" Annie's voice is hushed.

I feel too stunned to speak.

"He was just released. He served under seven years since he was a minor. Remember the trial?" Bruce looks at me. "Well, he came to apologize for what he'd done. Claimed he found religion while behind bars and yada-yada. I told him to leave us alone and never go near my family. I told him to go back to New York. He knew full well how serious I was, so I'm sure he took my advice."

"You're *sure* he took your advice?" I stare wide-eyed at him. "Bruce, that sounds awfully presumptuous, doesn't it? This isn't just some annoying neighbor you're asking to mind their own business; it's a hardened criminal."

"I know, I know." He nods wearily, "But he was a kid at the time, and he claims his brother pushed him into doing it, and… And I didn't know what else to do other than tell him to get out of town." His eyes light up, as if remembering something. "Well, actually I did call Lieutenant Bill Morton. He said don't worry about it, because if anything happens he'll handle it."

My eyes move towards Annie before I say anything, because I'm immediately worried about how she must be feeling about this, but her expression looks surprisingly unchanged. Although I guess it shouldn't be that surprising, considering she has always been strong minded. She speaks even before I get the chance to.

"Well, I don't know why you're letting it bother you, Dad. It's not that big of a deal. So what? He doesn't scare me and he shouldn't scare you."

After a moment of looking confused, this puts a small smile on Bruce's face. He nods awkwardly, picks up his fork, and starts to eat. I don't want to make a big deal of it or string out the conversation since I think we'd all rather think about something else, so I simply nod and agree with Annie.

"Yeah, don't worry about it. Good on you for telling him to get out of here. Thanks, hon. I'm sure if he doesn't take the hint then Bill will handle the rest."

"That he will. Bill takes things like this very seriously." Bruce nods, putting a spoonful of mashed potatoes into his mouth. He smiles at me as his cheeks puff out. I can't help but laugh, and when Annie looks up and notices her silly father with a mouthful of food, she joins in on the laughter.

"You look crazy, Dad." She shakes her head.

"Took too big of a bite," Bruce says, washing the potatoes down with a big gulp of water and then gasping. "That's me, silly ol' Dad. Always looking crazy." He winks at us and maintains eye contact with me for a moment and nods. We both share a silent moment together, a moment of relief. Everything is okay.

I'm glad he came clean about what was bothering him, and I'm glad that Annie managed to calm him down quickly by not making a big deal of it. That was a perfect example of a potentially stressful situation being deescalated. As I take a sip of wine I can't help but stare at Annie and feel proud of the woman she has turned into. Then I look at Bruce, watching him as he eats, and I smile as I think about how we managed to raise a pretty awesome young lady together.

Hearing that the man showed up at Bruce's work was undoubtedly startling, but Annie is right – *so what*? She's not scared of him, and we shouldn't be either. And besides, maybe his little gesture was genuine. Although that doesn't mean I'm going to accept it. He can say he's sorry all he wants – I'd rather him simply hit the road and get out of town. Out of sight, out of mind.

I don't want to see his face, because I know that would make me relive that horrible nightmare all over again. Poor Bruce, finding himself face to face with that little monster today. It makes me wonder... *Was* he being genuine with the apology? Did he travel all the way out here to the West Coast to apologize? That's... Odd.

And I'm not buying it.

I have to admit; the thought makes me kind of shiver a little bit. I don't want to think about why he came out here if not to genuinely apologize. Surely he isn't planning something. But if he tries anything, I'm sure Lieutenant Morton will handle the problem. He's a good Lieutenant, and I trust him to do his job well. Still, it makes me shudder to think that the man who kidnapped my daughter is right here in town now, breathing the same air as us… For so long now I've treated him and his brother as distant memories.

And now he's here in our town, possibly very close to us at this very moment.

I don't like that at all.

Chapter Fifteen
Annie

After dinner, I sit in bed and stare out my window at the dark streets below. Dad really caught me off guard, but I tried to play it cool. I'm sure he was probably worried about how I would feel after hearing what he had to say, but I don't want him to be worried about anything. I'm fine, really – just shocked. It's weird to think that my recent fears and anxieties seem to have come true. I didn't know exactly when he was getting out of jail, but I knew it was this year, so I don't know why I'm feeling so surprised that it actually happened. It was inevitable. But I guess it isn't just the fact that he's out. It's the fact that he's here.

Hearing that he'd officially been released would be one thing, but hearing that he came here to try to talk to my dad? That's another, and it's not the thing I expected to hear.

Oh well, there is nothing I can do about it. I can wish that it hadn't happened, that he had been released and had forgotten all about me after seven long years and moved on with his life, but that's not the reality of the situation, is it? So all I can do is hope that he won't come around anymore after Dad's warning. Let's hope he listens.

Dad and Mom are probably downstairs talking about it right now at the dinner table. I know they're talking about something, because I can hear their muffled voices even from up here in my bedroom on the second floor. I stand in my doorway and try to listen to what they're saying, but the words are too quiet to make out. That's okay, I guess. I could go downstairs and join in on the conversation if I really wanted to, but I guess the reason I came up here in the first place was because I felt overwhelmed with the thought of that man being here in San Francisco, and I didn't want to talk about it. And I definitely don't want to hear Mom and Dad talking worriedly about it, because I know that'll make me feel more anxious about it than I already feel.

I close my bedroom door and go to the bed. Then I pick up one of the books from the stack I got today at the used bookstore. Cracking it open, I feel a deep sense of relief coming over me as I flip to the first page and try to lose myself in the author's fictional world.

But I'm going to be honest, tonight I'm finding it harder than usual to do that.

Because I've got a lot of dark thoughts swirling around in my head, and I can't seem to shut them out.

Chapter Sixteen
Bruce

It's a funny thing, being a father. One minute you're raising your kid, helping them tie their shoes, helping to raise the spoon to their lips, teaching them words and teaching them things about life and not being afraid of things out of their control, and then the next minute they're grown adults and they're the ones calming *you* down and teaching *you* not to be afraid of things out of your control. It really is a funny thing.

I sit there on the edge of the bed thinking about that little fact as Judy comes out of the steaming bathroom wearing her robe.

"What's on your mind now?" She stops in her tracks and gives me a playful little side-eye.

I tell her. She chuckles and nods her head. "She's grown up, hasn't she? Now she's the one giving us advice."

I lie down on the bed and smile as Judy lies beside me. Her skin is hot to the touch from the shower. She runs her finger along my jaw and says, "Don't worry, Bruce. Our daughter's going to be just fine. I've been thinking about it, and I'm wondering if perhaps he *did* discover religion while locked up. Maybe he's a devout Christian now and felt the need to come apologize to you. I mean, I wish he hadn't bothered, but I suppose that's a lot better than the alternative being him simply coming here to taunt us passive aggressively..."

"I don't know. I hope he's being genuine. The smile on his face disturbed me."

"He was smiling? I imagined him looking nervous."

"Not nervous. Not much, at least. Maybe a little. He seemed confident, sure of himself, and about half a foot taller. Not to mention fifty or sixty pounds bigger, and most of that looked like hard, lean weight…"

"Well…"

"You know me, hon. I work out at the gym; I'm a pretty big guy. If he'd looked the same as he did about seven years ago, I'd have let out a breath and watched him tumble to the ground like a feather, but even I felt a little intimidated. He became a man while he was behind bars, and a big, strong one at that."

"Well, don't worry, honey. I know you worry yourself sick about Annie, but take her advice to heart. *Who cares*? He's not going to do anything. You think he wants to risk going back to prison? Even if he did come here to taunt you, it's probably as simple as that. Maybe he wanted to scare you and show off how big he'd gotten. He's not mentally all there in the first place considering the crime he and his brother committed."

"Oh, that reminds me," I say. "His brother's dead. I didn't bring that up to Annie because it just sounds kind of grim, you know? I didn't want to talk about prison shanking at the dinner table."

"Goodness. He was shanked?"

"Yeah. That's when they make a little homemade knife and-"

"Yeah, I know what it means, Bruce," she says.

"Is it bad I didn't feel sympathy when he told me that?"

"No," she says after a beat.

"I mean, how could I? After what they did. Especially the older one."

"Stop thinking about it, honey."

"Okay," I say softly.

I close my eyes and that's the last we speak of it, at least for the time being. Feeling my wife holding me makes me feel content and completely relaxed. It doesn't take long for me to drift off into a deep sleep.

The next morning we wake at our usual time, around six, and prepare for our work days. Annie has been working part time at a local live theater, but it's only three days a week. Today she is off, which means neither Judy nor I will see her by the time we leave the house at seven, as she will still be sound asleep.

I always leave some food for her in the refrigerator, though – boiled eggs, some bacon she can heat up if she likes, although I know she likes it crispy and cold, and Judy likes to cut up fruit and mix it in a bowl for her. We do this after eating our own breakfast together at the table. The early morning sun beams in through the dining room windows and illuminates Judy's beautiful face. It's times like these I truly realize how good I've got it in life. Not just because my wife is beautiful on the outside, but because she's the whole package. She's gorgeous both inside and out and she gave me the best daughter I could ask for. I love peaceful, simple little mornings spent sitting at the kitchen table, sipping my coffee and eating my eggs and bacon while I ponder about how good things have been going for me, and for us.

"See you, hon." Judy gives me a quick little peck on the side of my face as I finish loading the dishwasher. I turn and wrap my arms around her just as she starts to walk off. She stops and turns to face me as I hold her, smiling.

"Where's this affection coming from? I don't recognize this charming man."

"C'mon. I'm always charming," I say.

"Like this? I don't know about that."

"I'm always a little charming, aren't I? At least a little bit." I pinch my thumb and forefinger together and smirk.

"I got to get to work, silly." She kisses me again, this time on the lips. "Have a good morning."

"We still on for lunch at twelve thirty?"

"Yes, at Griffin's Diner."

"See you there."

I close the dishwasher and listen to it as it runs, standing there staring out the window as I watch Judy walking down the street. It's a gorgeous day in Northern California without a cloud in the sky and I feel like today is going to be very productive, which is always a good thing.

At the office I hold a meeting with one of my colleagues, Roy Nance. He sips coffee as we talk shop and then as he starts talking about the stock market I get up to pour myself another cup of coffee and glance out the window.

I do a double take and almost drop my coffee cup to the floor but instead I manage to just spill it all over my hand. "Ow!" I shout, setting the cup down on the table and wiping my hand as I glance back out the window.

"What is it? You okay?" Roy sits there looking confused.

"Yeah, I spilled coffee," I murmur, still gazing out the window, but no longer seeing the thing that caused me to spill the coffee in the first place.

I thought I'd seen him. I swear to God I saw him standing there on the corner by the crosswalk, arms crossed, face turned up towards the third floor window of my office. It's like he was looking right up at me. Then I looked down at the scalding coffee on my hands and when I looked back up a couple seconds later he was gone.

Come on. This is ridiculous. I must be imagining things. I'm just on edge from yesterday when he showed up, that's all. I'm sure of it. He didn't come back. That was probably just some young punk who looked like him. I turn back and stare at Roy.

"You sure you're okay?"

"Yeah, yeah, I'm fine. I just thought I saw somebody outside."

"Somebody who made you spill your coffee? What, you got a mistress now, Bruce? She stalking you?" He chuckles.

"That's very funny, Roy." I roll my eyes. Roy has always been a practical joker. The problem is, he is rarely as funny as he thinks he is.

"Seriously, though, who was it?" He raises an eyebrow as I sit back down with my half spilled cup of coffee.

"It was nobody, I guess. He wasn't there a second later when I looked again."

"He? Okay, so it's a *he*. Alright, that narrows it down to the male population of San Francisco. Make some business enemies lately, buddy? Want to be more specific about who this 'he' was? Maybe I could help you out. I'm good at strong arming people and putting a little scare into 'em." He laughs.

I lean away from the desk and stare up at the ceiling with my hands together, resting on my stomach. Then I look down at Roy and say, "Roy, did I ever tell you about the time my daughter was kidnapped?"

"Your daughter was kidnapped? Christy almighty, man. When?"

"Seven years ago in New York on the very first day of a family vacation." I turn and stare out the window as I lean back in the chair and reminisce. "She was taken for over two days by two men – well, one man and one minor – who demanded a ransom of a million dollars. Idiots. Dangerous idiots. I don't want to get into the details, but it worked out in the end with a bit of messy help from the police. For a moment there it seemed like it wasn't going to work out, though." I pause, staring off into space. "But it did."

"Jeez, man. I don't know what to say."

There is an uncomfortable silence in the room. I glance back at Roy and see him staring at me, nodding his head slowly, waiting for me to get to the point.

"Yesterday one of the men traveled to San Francisco and confronted me right in front of this building. Caught me way off guard. I wasn't prepared emotionally for that – I never thought I'd see him again. I hoped I wouldn't, at least."

"What? What are you talking about? He *confronted* you here? He's not in jail?"

"Was. He was released after serving six and a half years or so due to the fact that he was a minor. And I'm guessing he behaved himself behind bars and made as little of an impression as possible. The other one, the older brother, was killed in prison."

"Wow. This is a lot to take in, buddy." He swivels awkwardly in his seat. Roy isn't one for dark, serious conversations. He's all jokes and lightheartedness. I like Roy, even though his jokes don't often land. He's nice to have around and seems to brighten the mood. But right now I can tell I'm making him feel nervous. Not nervous about me, but nervous about what I'm telling him. "So, uh, what'd he say yesterday when he confronted you?" He asks eagerly.

"He said he came here from New York to apologize. He also wanted to apologize to Judy and Annie. I wasn't having any of that. I told him to never come around my family and to get out of town. I was pretty harsh about it too. At least I hope I was. I didn't want him to think I was just scolding him; I wanted him to know I meant it. I don't want to seem like a pushover, you know?"

"Yeah, of course."

"But I could've sworn I saw him standing down on the street corner just now, looking up at me."

"Sheesh." Roy rocks slowly in his chair with an anxious look on his face. Then he sits up awkwardly and walks slowly towards the window and turns back to me as if he is grappling with the frightening question of whether or not he wants to take a peek. He turns away from me and squats down, peering out.

"I don't see anybody. I mean, I see people walking past, but nobody standing there." A smile fills his face as he walks back to his seat and drops down into it with a heavy thud. "If you ask me, you might have yourself a bit of a problem here, Bruce."

"What do you mean?"

"I mean if you think you saw that fella down there staring up at the office, then you probably did. I've known you for four or five years now and you've always been levelheaded. You're not the type who sees things that aren't there."

"I should call the police," I say.

He nods towards the phone on the desk. "Yeah, I think that's a decent idea, buddy."

I feel myself breaking out into a cold sweat as I reach for the phone.

Chapter Seventeen
Judy

Over the years I've been fortunate to amass a growing number of clients. My original small studio I trained out of became a much larger studio, and with a larger studio came more machines, more dumbbells, more free weights, and more treadmills. I don't need a full size gym since I generally only train one client at a time, with the exception of couples, but it's nice to now have a variety of workouts I can put them through.

And with a growing number of clients comes a growing number of needs and personalities. Some clients like to be pushed with gentle, positive reinforcement. Others like to hear me practically scolding them like a drill sergeant.

As my ten o'clock appointment pushes through a grueling set of cable pulldowns I try my best to sound like the latter. "Two more reps. Come on; you've got that in you! Don't disappoint me."

She forces out the last two repetitions and gasps, wiping sweat from her forehead with a big towel strewn across her shoulder. I blush and look down at her. "I'm still trying to get used to talking like I'm some big meanie. You know that's not me at heart, right?" I laugh.

"I know. But trust me, it helps. I couldn't have got those last two reps without you yelling at me. That's why I need this. I won't progress without it."

She's training for an amateur bodybuilding competition. I train all sorts. Housewives who want to firm up a little, bodybuilders, powerlifters, elderly men and women who want to gain a little muscle in order to help longevity and quality of life, and husbands and wives who want to train together but don't know where to start. With each client comes the responsibility of learning how they need to be taught. I like the challenge, and so far I haven't had any bad reviews.

"That all for today?" She takes a big gulp from her water bottle and towel dries her face off again.

"Don't forget the last set of chest press. On the machine. Come on, Ruth."

"Aw," she says, laughing as she shakes her head. "I was trying to block it from my mind. I knew it was coming, though."

I get her to give me three good sets on the chest press machine, eight reps each – or however many she can push until she can't do another full rep. By the last set, she's hardly able to get seven, and when she finally does, her face is red and a big vein is bulging from her forehead. She sits there with her back up against the machine and breathes heavily, staring up at me with a smile on her face.

"*Now* we're done for the day."

"Now we're done for the day," I repeat. "Good job. I'll see you next time. Good luck at the competition."

"Thanks, Judy."

I walk her to the front doors of my studio and wave goodbye as she walks off down the street. Then I go get myself a glass of water in the small kitchen that sits nestled in the back right corner of my studio. Sometimes simply training *others* makes me feel like I've had a bit of a workout myself. Not usually, of course, but it feels like that when I'm training Ruth and the others who expect me to scream and be demanding. It's funny, to be honest, because that's so unlike my real personality, but I don't mind it because I know if I go easy on them then they won't give their maximum effort during their workouts.

I myself have been lucky in that I've never really felt the need to have any kind of trainer. I like working out alone, and being in there under the iron is enough to motivate me. Of course, I don't work out nearly as hard as Ruth does, because I have no interest in bodybuilding for myself, but I like the mental and physical benefits of building a bit of muscle, and I even find it pretty fun at times, despite the repetitive nature of it.

I figure I'll get in a little workout for myself now before it's time to rinse off in the shower and head to meet Bruce at Griffin's Diner, so I go over to the cables and start a quick but intense shoulder and arm workout, then after several sets of each muscle I move on to squats, doing four sets to near failure. After that, I feel like I've got legs made of jelly, and it's a challenge as I hobble into the shower and rinse off.

By twelve twenty five I'm walking into Griffin's and I eyeball Bruce sitting in the corner. He smiles at me and waves. It's nice to be able to have lunch with my husband. We don't do it that often, but once every month or two we make sure to. Despite the fact that he isn't a workaholic anymore, he still keeps himself pretty busy between the hours of nine to five, and to be honest, so do I. But I suppose that's a good thing, because we're both bringing in pretty good money at this point, and as long as those work hours don't start slipping past five o'clock into six and seven, then I don't mind a bit of hard work. Sometimes I've got to remind Bruce of that – to not work too late – but he's generally good about it these days, and I'm glad that we spend so much time together as a family now.

I sit across from him at the table and he smiles. "How's work?" He asks.

"Can't complain. I had a couple good clients today so far and got a few more scheduled after I get back to the studio. How about you, hon? You met with Roy, right?"

"Yeah, it's fine. Roy's good. He's staying busy with all the other little projects he's got going on. You know Roy, he's always working on something." He smiles and rubs his hand. I notice it's very red and looks almost burned.

"What happened to your hand?" I ask.

"Oh, that? It's nothing." He looks down at his hand and scoffs. "Silly old me spilled coffee on myself this morning. Piping hot coffee, at that."

"Oh, honey. Why'd you go and do something like that?" I frown, reaching over for his hand but realizing that I probably shouldn't touch it. It's not burnt badly, but it's noticeably red, and I know it must sting a bit.

Bruce chuckles and doesn't bother to say anything. I stare at him with a quizzical look and tilt my head to the side, wondering why he didn't answer the question. Maybe he thought it was rhetorical, but I don't think that's why he didn't answer. In fact, as he shuffles his hands around on the table and stares down at them, he looks a bit nervous, almost like he is hiding something from me. Or simply doesn't want to bother me with something that might make me worry.

"Bruce?"

"It was something stupid," he says at last, waving it off.

"Well, tell me, hon. I'm your wife."

"I don't want to bother you with it."

I knew it.

I smile and shake my head. "Come on, honey. You're not bothering me with anything. If someone sees their spouse with a burnt hand and they say they spilled coffee all over it, they're going to wonder what happened. I mean, are you okay?"

"I'm fine. I just thought I saw the guy again."

I hesitate, thinking it over. *The guy?*

I'm hoping, of course, that he isn't referring to the man I'm thinking about, but in my heart, I know he is. I shudder a little and Bruce seems to notice.

"Honey, it's okay. I think I was just imagining – I mean, I wasn't imagining it, but I think I was just mistaken. It was someone else I saw. I'm pretty sure of it."

"You're pretty sure of it."

"I couldn't swear on it, but I don't think it was him now that I've thought it over."

"But you thought it was him initially. And it shocked you enough to make you spill your coffee all over your hand."

"Yeah," he says softly, lowering his gaze to his hand. He peers up at me again and smiles reassuringly. "But listen, like I said, I think I was wrong. But you know what? Just to be safe, I called the cops again. Bill Morton was out, but I talked to someone else, a Walton or a Walter, I can't remember – anyway, they sent a cop to come drive by my office, and I didn't hear any news back, so no news is good news. Right?"

"I hope so," I say. I suddenly feel weird. A deep sense of worry has come over me. I'm anxious about what Bruce has told me.

I feel like I sense a desperation in his voice as he tells me that he thinks he was wrong, and that he saw someone else. It's almost as if he's trying to calm me down a little because he doesn't want me to worry. But I wish he would just be straight with me, because I need to know if he really thinks he saw the man or not.

"Bruce, do you really think it wasn't him?"

That question wipes the smile off his face. He blinks several times as he stares at me and shrugs, then lets out a long sigh. "To tell you the truth, I don't know what I think. I feel like I'm just trying to talk myself into believing that it wasn't him, because I don't want it to have been him. Oh, hell, honey, seven years ago was a long time, but ever since I saw his face yesterday I feel like all those horrid memories have just come back and I've felt so overwhelmed. I don't know what to do now. If he's here and he starts stalking us, I'm going to be livid. I'm sure the cops will be able to handle it if that's the case, but my worst fear is that he's discreet about it. What if he's hard to catch? What if he just shows up at random? What if he's watching us at times when we don't even notice it?"

"Bruce, you're kind of frightening me," I say uneasily.

"I'm sorry, honey. I didn't mean to." He reaches over and puts his red, tender looking hand over mine.

The waitress comes at that moment and takes our orders. I get a turkey sandwich with fries on the side and Bruce gets a double cheeseburger with bacon. When she walks off I take a long breath and glance out the window, half expecting to see that creep standing there on the sidewalk looking in at us. But I don't, fortunately, and I remind myself that I'm going to slip into a paranoid state if I'm not careful. And so will Bruce – he's even worse about it than me, I think. When he gets worked up about something, he *really* gets worked up. I love him, but he's not as strong as I am mentally. Sure, he's a fairly big guy who can handle himself physically, but I know that during times of stress, he's always in worse shape than I am.

I put my hands gently over his and smile. "It's going to be okay, honey. If you *did* see this guy again today, then so what? So he's stalking us. That's creepy, yeah, but maybe he's being genuine about what he told you. Maybe he wants to apologize. We'll let him try that until the police show up at the right time. Then they'll arrest him for stalking, or if they feel nice, they'll warn him and tell him to get lost before they *do* arrest him the next time. It'll play out like that. You know? So quit worrying because the truth is nothing's going to come of this. Nothing bad's going to happen. Annie's going off to college in the fall, you and I are doing wonderful with our careers and our relationship, and everything is going good. Let's not let this little weirdo ruin that for us just because he's trying to pry himself back into our lives. We're not going to *let* him do that, okay?"

Bruce nods his head. The muscles in his face seem to have relaxed a bit. *Good job,* I tell myself. *You're managing to calm your worry-wart husband down a bit. That's a job well done.*

"I needed to hear that," he says. He smiles at me.

I'm glad I made him feel better by saying that.

Everything is going to be fine. A situation may have arisen with this creep being here in town, but

we're on top of it, at least. The cops are aware of it and nothing bad is going to happen.
    That's what I tell myself, at least.

Chapter Eighteen
Bruce

Here I am, supposedly the man of the house, the big, tough father figure who should be unafraid and telling my wife and daughter that everything is going to be okay. And yet at this moment I feel like I'm the one who's in need of encouragement from *them*. First Annie made me feel better during dinner by brushing off my concerns about the man showing up, and now today at lunch my wife did the same thing in her own way.

I've got it made. I really do. I've got the best wife and the most wonderful daughter a man could ask for, and if there is one thing this whole situation has given me over the years, it's an ever deeper appreciation for my family than I already had. And now with him showing up again in our life, or trying to, at least, I'm feeling closer and more protective of them than ever. I won't let anything happen to them. I wouldn't dare let him get close to my daughter again. Not after what happened before. I couldn't fail like that as a father.

I remember the feeling I had back then, seven years ago. The feeling of failing. The feeling of complete hopelessness as I sat in that hotel suite in Midtown Manhattan, staring down at the snowy city, dreading the call I thought we inevitably were going to receive at any moment – the call telling us that our daughter was found.

Found *dead*.

But that call never came. Still, it was two days of misery, two days of waiting for a handoff that I thought would solve nothing. And I still shudder as I think about the handoff and how that played out; how it almost backfired on us. How it almost got the three of us killed. I remember the moment the blindfolds were put on, then the moment I heard Tony gasping, followed by the sound of the police screaming from the street. I remember the feeling of sheer panic raining down on me as I thought to myself: *The cops blew it. They didn't anticipate the kidnappers asking us to get into the vehicle with them. Why hadn't we thought of that? They blew it big time, and so did I. I should have anticipated this. But I didn't. And now we're going to die.*

I still feel chills when I remember what it felt like to have my hands wrapped completely around the man's throat as I squeezed like my life depended on it. I guess it did. We were fighting to the death. I was trying to kill him. It's the only time in my life I can say I've ever tried to kill anyone. And if there had been ten or fifteen more seconds before the crash, maybe I would have.

I hope that's the last time I ever have to try to kill someone.

I'm not a violent person by any means. In fact – and I'm slightly embarrassed to admit this – I've never been in any kind of scuffle or physical confrontation in my life. I guess the reason I'm embarrassed to admit that is because it makes me feel less 'manly,' but I know that's silly. Still, that time in the van is the only time I've had to use force against someone. I wonder if I'll ever have to use force like that again? The thought makes me feel ill. The last thing I'd want to do is hurt someone, but if I have to, then I will.

For instance, if someone happened to come after my daughter again, or if they came after my wife. In a situation like that, I wouldn't hesitate. I wouldn't even have to think about it. I'd be acting on instincts in a scenario like that, and I don't think that's a unique viewpoint. I think most anyone would react physically if the people they loved were being hurt.

Come on. Why are you dwelling on this? I shake my head as I stare out at the street below. I close the blinds and sigh, turn, and walk back to my desk. It's four o'clock and I'm all alone in my office now. I fill out some dull reports, check some business emails, and then lean back in my seat and toss a tennis ball up and down, catching it in my hand and slinging it up at the ceiling over and over.

Well, I think my work day is over. Not much else to do right now, since I've finished up with all the tasks I had on today's date on the calendar.

I get up, stretch, and grab my coat from the coat rack. Then I open the door, turn to lock it, and stroll down the hall towards the elevator. After I go through the front doors I step onto the sidewalk, walk down to the corner, turn, and almost jump out of my skin when I bump into him.

"Oh, Mr. Hurt. Sorry to scare you, sir."

"What the hell are you doing here?" I shout, taking several steps back and wiping the hair from my forehead. I've already begun to sweat and my face feels hot. I can feel my heart thundering in my chest as he stares at me like a deer in headlights.

"What?" He says defensively. "I was staying at a hotel nearby and I was going to the corner store for a bite to eat."

"What are you doing in town still?" I raise a finger and try to look intimidating. I'm almost certain that I'm failing.

"I didn't have a whole lot of money when I got out. It cost me quite a bit to get here, sir. I'm trying to find a way to get back, but in the meantime, it looks like I'm stuck here in town."

"No, no, no – you're not. You're not stuck here." I step towards him now, cornering him against the brick wall of my office building. Sweat trickles down my nose and hangs from the tip. I hold my finger towards him. "Stop feeding me lies. Stop *messing* with me, or I swear, you're going to regret it." I pause, glaring at him without allowing myself to blink. "Now here's what you're going to do. You're going to get on the next flight out of town. I don't care where you go as long as it's outside the state lines. And guess what? You probably expect me to tell you that I'm not going to call the police as long as you leave. Well, that's where you're wrong." I reach into my pocket and pull my phone out. Then I dial Lieutenant Bill Morton and press the phone to my ear. I smile. He smiles back at me innocently, as if he thinks I'm just giving him a hard time and it's all fun and games.

"Hi Bill," I say after hearing him come onto the line. I try not to let my voice shake, but I'm swimming with emotions. "I'm standing here with the man I told you about. He's still stalking me. He's right outside my office again, just around the corner of the building. Says he's staying at a hotel nearby. Was hoping you'd be able to swing by and have a chat with him. He's being a bit too hardheaded for me. Maybe you could get the point across better."

"I'm about ten minutes away. Think he'll stay there?"

I stare into Tony's eyes and try to read his face. He's still got the wide eyes and the innocent smile on his face, like he can't figure out why I'm angry at him. Is he that stupid, or is it all an act?

"I don't know," I mutter. "Just get here as soon as you can, Bill. Thanks." I put my phone back in my pocket. "Police are on their way, and they're going to love talking to you, I'd be willing to wager."

His lips start quivering as he stares at me. Then he turns his eyes to the ground and shakes his head. "I was just trying to do the right thing, sir. I was trying to make it right with you and your family. I hope you'll at least be willing to tell them I'm sorry for me if you won't let them hear it from my lips."

"They'll absolutely never hear it from your lips. I told you you'd better stay away from my family."

"Or else," he says, and looks back up at me.

I stare at him uneasily; taken aback by the look he's giving me now. The smile has disappeared from his face, and he is glaring at me even harder than I'm glaring at him. But then the smile pops right back up on his face like a light being turned on, and he shakes his head and laughs very softly as he waves his hand gently in the air.

"I'll leave you be, Mr. Hurt. You and your family, I'll leave you all alone. I'll leave town by bus tonight. I can't promise you that I'll be able to make it past state lines by midnight, but I'll try my hardest to appease you, because it's clear to me that I've upset you, and that's not something I want to do. I didn't intend to make you angry, Mr. Hurt. My intention was genuine; my coming here to apologize to you and yours. Again, I'm sorry. Please give my apology to your wife and daughter. In particular, please tell your daughter that I'm very sorry for my actions and that I feel a lot of regret. Tell her I learned a lot in prison and spent most of the time reading books. Through those books I learned a lot about myself and became a better person, and-"

"Shut up," I say, poking his chest so hard that he tries to move away. I keep him cornered. "Just shut up. I don't want to hear your lousy apologies, and I don't want to hear your life story. I don't care about you or what you have to tell me. Just get out of town now. Or better yet, why not stick around for a few minutes and talk with my friend from downtown at the police station? How about that?" I raise an eyebrow and grin at him, trying to scare him.

It seems to work. His lip starts quivering and he turns on his feet and scurries off like the rat he is. I kick the sidewalk and laugh, yelling after him, "Don't come back. You come back and I'll have you arrested before you step foot off the bus. I've got connections downtown within the police force." This isn't exactly true; save for one connection, which is Lieutenant Bill Morton. Other than that, I don't even know any of the officers by name.

He turns the corner and is gone. I honestly wish he'd stuck around for a while longer. I really would have liked seeing Bill rough him up a bit or at least scare him. But to be honest, I think I did a pretty good job of scaring him myself. I smile at the thought, feeling a little proud of myself.

"Not bad, Bruce," I say, chuckling.

I did good just now. And I'm sure I won't see him again.

In fact, I'll bet he's halfway to the bus station already.

Chapter Nineteen
Annie

Heather slings a chip into her mouth and squints as she holds up her hands. "Wait, wait. You're telling me this guy showed up at your dad's work? Three thousand miles away? And it was just to apologize, he said?"

"Yeah, apparently."

"That's, um, kind of creepy," her voice drones monotonously. She grabs her soda and sips on it, shaking her head.

We're sitting in the desolate food court of a shopping plaza, and I've just told her everything, starting from the beginning. She already knew about how I was kidnapped as a kid – her and Nancy are two of my only friends I'm still in contact with who know – but I never told her all the details about it. I never felt comfortable reliving it, but now I'm telling her everything, just because I want her opinion.

She frowns. "I don't think he's genuinely here to apologize. I don't want to scare you though. It's not like I think he's gonna try to kidnap you again, or something dumb like that. I bet he just came here to try and scare your dad. He probably blames him for going to jail and for his brother being killed." She cocks her head to the side and makes a face. "But I'm not a professional detective, or anything close to it, so take my opinion with a grain of salt." A smile fills her face as she tosses another potato chip into her mouth and reaches for her soda once more.

I nod and think it over. What she is saying definitely makes more sense than what he claims to have come here for. Traveling three thousand miles to apologize to the father of the daughter you kidnapped seven years ago… Yeah, that just sounds like complete baloney. I don't buy it, and I know Dad doesn't buy it. I shrug and start eating my burger. Heather's already finished hers, but I didn't have much of an appetite as I told the story, so it just sat on the table getting cold. But now that I've told her everything there is to tell and heard her opinion, it feels like my appetite has come roaring back.

I take a big bite of the burger and say, "I think you're right. Either way, he's apparently gone now. Or so he says."

"Yeah. Sounds like your dad scared him off last night. Hopefully, I mean. That's creepy how he was outside his work again."

"He said he was getting some food at the corner store near his hotel. He claimed to be staying nearby. But yeah, it's weird. Really weird. I hope he meant it when he said he was leaving. Dad didn't seem to be too concerned about it anymore last night. He smiled as he sat at the dinner table for about thirty minutes straight, looking as proud as I've ever seen him."

"That's too funny." Heather smirks as she finishes her bag of chips and crumbles it up in her hands. She washes it down with some more soda and leans forward. A serious expression comes over her face, or maybe it's not so serious after all, because I see a little grin start to appear at the edge of her mouth. I always have a hard time reading her. She's always so deadpan when speaking. "What if the guy was lying, though? Like, what if he shows up *right now* here in the food court? What would you do?"

"That's not a nice thing to imagine," I say.

"Sorry," she says. "Didn't mean to scare you. You know me, I just like horror movies, so naturally my imagination is going to go there… But, I mean, what if? What if he really starts stalking you?" She lifts an eyebrow and peers at me from under it.

"He's gone, I think," I say. "Said he was taking a bus out of town last night. So, I think stalking is probably out of the question. *Probably*." I smile, trying to make light of it all.

"Yeah, that's what he said, alright. He said he was going to leave. Uh-huh." Heather looks down at her hands and exhales softly, then mutters under her breath, "But criminals like him aren't exactly known for being very trustworthy, are they?" Her eyes move back up to my face. "I mean, can you trust that sort of person?"

I glare at her a little. "You keep saying you're trying not to scare me, but you've definitely managed to freak me out a little bit. Nice going." I laugh.

"Sorry." She says again, leaning back. "God, I always do this, don't I? I always say the wrong thing." She blushes a little, gently smacking her forehead with the palm of her hand. "I'm such a klutz sometimes. I'm always too morbid about things."

"It's okay. I'll still be your friend," I joke.

"Thanks for always being patient with me. I know I'm hard to deal with sometimes." She rolls her eyes and laughs.

"It's okay. I'm used to it."

We laugh. Even with her managing to scare me a little (supposedly unintentionally), I still can't help but feel like I'm having fun when I'm sitting with Heather. I guess it's just something about the way she speaks so lackadaisically about such dark, frightening subjects like being stalked by my former kidnapper. The monotonous tone of her voice never fails to make me chuckle, even when the subject matter is grim. I can never take her seriously, even when we're talking about serious topics such as this.

But I hope she's wrong about the thing she brought up – the possibility of him not really leaving town after all. And needless to say, I hope he isn't stalking me. But I don't think he is. From what Dad says, the guy was pretty startled last night. I guess Dad caught him off guard with how angry he got, and by calling the police right in front of him. From what Dad said, it sounds like the guy ran away. Honestly, it's kind of funny to imagine.

I smile as we sit there sipping soda, chit-chatting about this and that. We've moved onto lighter topics, like movies, books, funny cat videos, and where we see ourselves in five years. Things like that. Things that we always talk about.

We stand up and take our trays to the trashcan, then walk through the shopping center and head for the front doors. The sun is beaming through the glass, and I squint as I step out into the bright day with Heather beside me. We plan on going to watch a movie later in the afternoon. After that, we'll probably stop somewhere for ice cream. I'll miss my friend when we both go off to college. Sadly, we're going to different universities, but at least we'll be in the same state.

As I walk down the street listening to Heather talking about her boyfriend I don't think anything of the man in the long black rain coat passing by us. Not until he's already passed and turned the corner. But suddenly I freeze and let out a loud gasp as I turn my head, feeling my heart bouncing between my ribcage like a basketball. Heather stops talking and stares at me.

"What is it?" She says, wide-eyed and scared.

I glance down the street and take several steps to look around the corner. The man is gone. I could have sworn it was him, but maybe it was just my imagination. I wasn't really paying attention, and it didn't register until a moment later. Maybe it was because we were just talking about him – maybe that's why my mind was playing tricks on me. Maybe I'm just paranoid.

Maybe.

"Nothing," I say, shaking my head. "I just thought I saw someone. But it couldn't have been him – this guy was a lot bigger."

Heather stares at me anxiously and looks back and forth down the street, spinning slowly on the soles of her sneakers.

A strong breeze blows past us, and I suddenly feel very cold and all alone on this quiet street.

Chapter Twenty
Judy

The mouthwatering aroma of chili coming from the kitchen radiates all the way upstairs where I lie in bed reading a book. Bruce is making dinner tonight, and I'm glad, because he makes the best chili I've ever had the pleasure of sitting down and eating. And I certainly can't wait to sit down and eat the batch he's whipped up tonight. I'm halfway tempted to toss my book onto the nightstand and hurry downstairs now, but I know if I do he'll say what he always says: "It's not ready yet. It needs to sit for a while longer. Let's let the flavor marinate for a bit, hon."

He's so lovably predictable in his ways, so I know to wait here patiently in bed until he calls for me. I bury my nose back in my paperback, feeling my stomach rumble, until I hear the front door open. That must be Annie; I'm glad she's decided to come home early enough to eat with us. I know she planned on being out with Heather today.

This morning was a bit stressful because Bruce wasn't sure if he was okay with that, considering that awful man from our past had shown up in town and all. And even though the man claimed to be leaving last night by bus, Bruce still felt nervous about letting Annie out of the house without one of us with her. But of course, she's an adult now and she can do what she wants, even though she still seems like a kid to us. I told her to please be careful and to stay in very public areas. I also told her to text me throughout the day, which she did, albeit a bit reluctantly. Deep down I knew the idea of her getting kidnapped again seven years later was a bit ludicrous, even if the man was still here in San Francisco. It would be like lightning striking twice.

Or maybe that's just me being a naïve, overly optimistic parent. The thought distracts me from my reading, and I set my book down on the nightstand and sigh. Well, she is home now, so I guess I wasn't being too optimistic after all. I slide off the bed and head downstairs where the scent of chili is much stronger. It's a pleasant scent, to say the least, and it makes my stomach rumble noisily.

"What was that *noise*?" Annie asks as I walk into the living room.

I raise a hand and laugh. She looks over at me and squints. "Holy cow, Mom, that was your stomach? Did you skip lunch today or something?"

"No. Your father's chili always makes my appetite go haywire. I think it's the smell. It makes me feel like I haven't eaten in days. I go crazy for it."

"Well, you'd better save some for Annie and me," Bruce says teasingly as he walks into the room behind me and wraps his arms around me for a quick hug and kiss on the cheek. "I'm kidding. Dinner's ready, girls," he says.

"Woo-hoo," Annie exclaims as she hops up from the couch and hurries past us.

I turn to Bruce and smile at him. Then I give him a quick kiss on the lips. "Thanks for dinner, hon. You know I love when you make chili."

"I do it for you." He shrugs.

We walk into the kitchen and pour big bowls of chili for ourselves. I smile as I sit across from Annie, who devours her bowl like she's even hungrier than I am.

"Talk about skipping lunch…" I give her a curious look.

She grins sheepishly. "Heather and I were going to have ice cream after the movie, but she had to skip it because she's meeting with her sister in Berkley." She pauses. "I did have lunch, though. I guess Dad's chili just has the same effect on me as it does you." She chuckles.

"I think it has that effect on everyone."

Like mother like daughter. And like father too, for that matter – Bruce is digging in to his chili, practically inhaling it. For as hungry as I am, I feel like I'm the only one eating with any sort of table manners. I don't mind, though, and in fact I find it funny. I love my family – both Annie and Bruce are a hoot to live with, and I'll miss her when she goes off to UCLA in the next couple of months.

"I thought I saw the guy today," she says casually, catching me off guard. Bruce looks over at her and then his eyes move towards me for a fleeting moment before turning back to Annie.

"The guy?" He says sharply.

"You know. The *tour guide*." She enunciates the words as if they're a joke, then shakes her head. "The creep who kidnapped me when I was a little girl. But it wasn't him. I mean, it couldn't have been. This guy was a lot bigger. It was just that when I saw his face, I thought for a second that it was him."

"Jesus, Annie. Where did you see him? Where was it?" Bruce asks quickly. His face goes red and he clenches both fists together on the table.

"What?" She stares at him. "What's wrong? It wasn't him, right? I mean, he was a lot heavier. I just thought it looked like his face at first but then realized it couldn't have been him."

"The guy's put on a lot of size. His physique looks unrecognizable" Bruce sighs, rubbing his head. He chews on his upper lip as he looks at me with worry behind his eyes.

"So it was him," Annie says softly, putting down her spoon.

"Yeah, honey. It was probably him. Oh, this is just *wonderful*." Bruce rubs his temples, stands up from the table, and walks over to the countertop. He leans on it, hunched over with his back to us. "God, I'm a fool for taking his word. I should have known he'd stick around. I feel like a grade-A moron for thinking he'd be on a bus out of here. I should have known." He turns and gazes at Annie with a wired look in his eyes. "Did he *look* at you, Annie? He must've been following you."

"I don't know," she says softly; her voice is almost a whisper. "I just saw him pass by. It happened so fast. I wouldn't have even noticed him if I hadn't looked up."

Slowly, Bruce shakes his head from side to side. "Oh, this makes me sick. It makes me livid. He's screwing with us. He was *that* close to you, and…" He closes his mouth and stares down at the ground for a moment before jerking his head back up to stare at us. "I was right to be nervous this morning. I shouldn't have let you go out, Annie. That was reckless of me. It was *stupid*, that's what it was. Christ, I'm going to wind up getting my daughter kidnapped again, aren't I? This is just *wonderful* news. And here I was thinking he'd left the state."

"Bruce, please don't get angry," I say.

"I'm not angry at you," he says quickly, waving his hand through the air. "I'm not angry at either of you." His voice is low now, and he stares down at his feet before looking up at us. "I'm just angry at myself. I'm angry at my poor judgment. I can't believe he was even within eyesight of you, Annie. I can't forgive myself for allowing that to happen."

"Dad, it's okay. It's not your fault. I just turned the corner and saw him passing by. I think it was a coincidence. San Francisco isn't all that big, you know."

"No, that's not it. It wasn't a coincidence," he says slowly, gazing at her. He pulls out his cell phone and sighs. "We need to tell the police. I know I already told Bill Morton, but we've got to make an official report now down at the station. I think that might help. Maybe." He puts his phone back in his pocket and sighs. "We'll go down there after dinner and do this in person. No more games, no more warnings. I want them to bring this guy down. Surely he's breaking parole by doing this, right? I mean, for God's sake, he's got to be doing something illegal by being here, don't you think?" He stares at me with a desperation in his eyes, which I haven't seen in a long time. "They didn't just let him come out to California to stalk us after releasing him, did they? There's got to be some kind of rule he's breaking."

"I don't know, Bruce," I say. "But I don't think breaking the law is something he's too worried about."

Chapter Twenty-One
Bruce

Clenching the wheel, I steer the car quietly through the city streets as I try to silently reassure myself that this is all going to blow over soon. Judy is in the passenger seat, with Annie sitting in the back, and they both are just as silent as I am. The mood is somber as we ride towards the police station. Once we get there, I ask for Lieutenant Morton, but as I suspected, he already went home at five. Now it's eight, and we're directed instead to someone ranked even higher than Morton, a Captain Hank Wilcox. He is a heavyset man with a bushy gray mustache over a set of thin, pursed lips. His eyebrows are almost just as thick as the mustache, and they rest above a set of thoughtful looking eyes as blue as the Caribbean. He greets us with a gruff mumble and a nod of his head.

"C'mon in." He motions for us to join him in his office, where he sits down behind a big oak desk and props his feet up on it. Then, running his fingers along his mustache, he surveys us with a blank face; his eyes wandering from me, to Annie, to Judy, and then settling back on me. He crosses his arms together and speaks. "So, you're friends with Bill?"

"Yeah, we go back a ways," I say.

"Good man." He yawns, then reaches for a small cup of coffee on his desk. "Coffee?" He motions towards a pot over on a table near the window.

"No thanks. We're okay," I say.

He sips from his cup and then holds it on his stomach, resting it there with both hands clasped around it. "Okay, folks. What seems to be the problem?"

Judy and I go over the entire story from top to bottom, beginning with our trip seven years ago to Manhattan up to the most recent development with Annie seeing the man on the street. Once we have finished speaking, Captain Wilcox runs the tip of his tongue along his lip, going over it repeatedly in a circle as if he is deep in thought. Then he sets his coffee cup on the table and leans forward, propping his elbows up on it.

"I can get in touch with New York and see if he's in violation of some type of parole. I'm certain he is. That's the way it works in situations like this. There are always conditions to a release; rules that must be followed. He could be busted on parole violation."

"What if you all can't find him?"

"Well, we'll try our best is all I can say."

Judy nods her head and glances at me before looking back to Captain Wilcox. "What can we do?"

"In the meantime?" He frowns. "Just live your life – with some extra caution, that is. I'd recommend not going out late at night for walks, just to err on the safe side. We're talking about a potentially dangerous criminal here, despite the man's claims that he's found God and wants mere forgiveness." He lets out a deep chuckle and takes another sip of coffee. "In my opinion, the man may want just that, as silly as it may sound."

"You mean, you believe him?" My brow furrows.

"I don't know. He could be a liar, or he could have really convinced himself that he did something wrong and managed to change while incarcerated. So he may not be a threat to you if that's the case. Creepy and annoying, but not a threat. If my suspicions are correct, he very well may have traveled here to do exactly what he told you – to apologize. Still, that doesn't mean he isn't in violation of parole…" His coarse mustache rises up as he grins. "So, you folks won't need to worry about him badgering you much longer. He'll be arrested on that. Once we speak to New York and confirm the conditions of his release, we'll act swiftly on finding him. He'll face some serious charges once he's back in New York."

"But what if you all can't find him?" Annie says suddenly.

Captain Wilcox's eyes dart over to where she sits beside us. He gives her a little smile. "We'll try our best. But don't worry too much about that. We're pretty good at finding people who need to be found."

"I hope so, Captain," I say.

He looks at me and smirks. "What's on your mind? Worried about how well the San Francisco Police Department can operate? I know, every force has its problems, but believe me, if this man is still in town, we'll be able to locate him. It might take a bit of time, but we'll be able to locate him. So don't worry.

We'll have this little problem of yours solved soon enough."

I can tell that the captain's heart is in the right place. He seems like a good man, similar to Lieutenant Morton, and I like how proactive he sounds. My biggest fear while driving down here to the station was that we would meet a bored, disinterested cop who rushed us through our story and then told us there was nothing that could be done about the problem. Captain Wilcox is the opposite of that. He seems engaged with what we're telling him, and motivated to find this little nuisance and arrest him.

But the problem is I don't exactly buy into his confidence. And I'm really struggling to accept the idea of this man coming here to simply beg for our forgiveness.

What if he came here for revenge?

Chapter Twenty-Two
Annie

I feel strange as we leave the police station and get back into Dad's car. I want to say I feel overwhelmed, but that isn't really the right word to describe it. In some ways I feel sort of numb, like a lot of things have begun to happen that I have no control over, and so I've just come to the conclusion that I have to accept whatever happens. It feels like that with this man being in town, this fake tour guide – it feels like he's here to stay and despite what the police captain said, there isn't really anything we can do about it.

He said they would be able to find him quickly, but I've got a bad feeling they might be wrong about that. I don't know why I'm feeling so negative about this, though. It was only a couple nights ago that I was telling my dad not to worry about it, and now here I am, feeling just as worried as him. He and Mom are so quiet as we ride home, and I don't bother saying anything either. I don't think any of us feel particularly talkative right now. I'm sure we all just want this problem to go away.

It's only been a couple of days since he showed up, though, so maybe we're making a bigger deal of this than it really is. It's not like he's going to stick around town for long. That just isn't feasible, not with us having notified the cops. Plus, Captain Wilcox said he's going to alert New York. I'm sure he's right about this man violating his parole. But I guess the question is – does that matter? If he's here in town, then he's well aware of the fact that he is violating parole. What difference would that make for him? None, I guess, but at least it would make a difference for the police, because they would be able to arrest him then for breaking the law.

Dad finally speaks as we get close to our house. "Everything is going to be okay," he says. He turns up onto our street and pulls into the garage. Then, after cutting the engine, he turns and looks at Mom and me. "You two don't worry about a thing, okay? I've reported this creep to Bill at least twice now, and now we've reported it with the captain. Things are going to start moving quickly now and they'll find the guy. I'm positive." He gives me what I suspect is supposed to be an encouraging smile, but it doesn't encourage me much, because I can see the nervousness behind his eyes.

We walk out of the garage and start for the front door, but then, just as Dad opens the gate for the front steps, a man appears from behind a bush and stands there in the darkness. Dad lets out a stunned gasp and takes a step back, blocking Mom and me from the man with his arms outstretched.

As if that is going to stop the hulking figure who looms before us.

"I just want to talk to you," he says, clasping his hands before his chest as if in prayer. "Why won't you let me talk to you? I was just a kid. I was sixteen years old and you're acting like I was a grown man. I didn't even understand the gravity of what I was doing. It was my brother who talked me into doing it. He basically made me do it. I just want to apologize. I've got to make amends or else I can't live with myself. Why won't you believe me? Don't you realize that prison can change a person?" His voice quavers as he stands there with his arms outstretched, his hands clenched together.

    Then he begins to walk towards us.

Chapter Twenty-Three
Judy

Tony beelines in our direction. "All I ask is that you hear me out and believe me when I say I've changed," he says.

It happens very quickly. One second he's five feet away from us, ranting and raving about how he just wants to apologize, and then the next second it's as if he's decided he's going to get up close and personal with us – as if *that's* going to convince us. Before I get a chance to even consider what we should do, I watch with shock as Bruce sends a fist flying up into Tony's jaw, causing him to topple backwards onto the sidewalk. He lands with a thud and rolls several feet down the hilly street before bumping into a parked sedan.

It's the first time I've ever seen my husband get into an altercation with someone else on the street. I think he is just as shocked as I am. He stands there holding his fist up, gazing at it like it's a weapon he never knew existed. Then he looks at me with startled eyes and his mouth hanging open, but only for a second, because his attention quickly goes back to the man lying on the ground. He rushes over towards him as Tony has begun pulling himself to his feet, and he grabs him by the front of his shirt, pulling him closer as he throws another punch.

And another.

As Bruce sends a series of swift, brutal punches into Tony's midsection, Tony doubles over and grunts with pain. He doesn't bother to attempt to fight back. He seems to have no interest in even defending himself by raising his arms. He just stands there hunched over, taking each and every hit until he collapses to the ground.

There is something disturbingly self-destructive about the way he accepts the blows. It's as if he takes the punches because he feels like he deserves them.

Bruce stands there sweating and breathing harder than I've ever seen him breathe. He stares down at Tony, who lies there panting, gazing up at Bruce with a broken and bloodied face. Bruce waves a stern finger at him and begins to stumble backwards, dizzy and undoubtedly exhausted. At this point I reach into my pocket and grab my phone. I dial 911 and hold it to my ear. When the dispatcher answers, I tell them our address and the situation. They tell me they're sending a car.

Tony coughs violently on the ground and tries to stand up before collapsing again. He groans from where he lies and then rolls over onto his back for a moment before managing to twist himself back over onto his stomach. He tries to stand again, but it's too difficult for him to do so.

"I told you," Bruce says. "I warned you. And next time I'll kill you."

Tony coughs violently again and rubs his bloodied lip. He looks up at Bruce and frowns, shaking his head. "I swear, I just wanted your forgiveness. I had to ask for it in person. I couldn't live with myself if I didn't at least try once I got released." He reaches up to wipe his lip again. Then he pulls himself to his feet and almost falls back down to the ground but manages to catch himself on the hood of a car. He looks at me, at Bruce, and then at Annie. His eyes finally seem to settle on her, gazing fixedly in her direction. "I'm so sorry for taking you that day. You were just a kid. It was my brother's idea, but I take some of the blame too. I should have known better. You didn't deserve that. Nobody would deserve to live through that fear, trapped in a dark room waiting to find out if you were going to live or die. We just wanted the money, that's all. But I know it must have been hell for you to experience that. I'm so sorry. I hope you'll forgive me."

"Shut up." Bruce walks towards him. "Don't you dare speak to my daughter."

Tony holds up his arms in front of his face and winces. "Please, no more. I'm done. I've said my piece. I've said what I came here to say."

Sirens wail in the distance. Tony looks back towards the sound and then at us, shaking his head. "You'll never see me again. I promise. Please don't live in fear of me coming back because I won't. I'm finished. I've said my piece. I'm sorry. Goodbye."

He turns and breaks into a limping run, groaning with pain as he rushes down the street and then turns the corner. The sound of police sirens grows louder. Bruce sits down on the sidewalk and crosses his legs, waiting for them to arrive. Annie and

I stand by each other, staring down the street as the red and blue lights appear around the corner.

Chapter Twenty-Four
Bruce

Two months later...

I crack open a bottle of sparkling water as I stand by the side of the moving van and smile as Annie walks out from the front doors of her dorm. I can't believe two months have passed, and now it's time for our daughter to go away all on her own.

"Thanks, Dad. I still can't believe you offered to drive all my stuff all the way from San Francisco. You didn't have to do that."

"Hey, it beats hiring expensive movers. You know me, I'm cheap," I joke, nudging her shoulder. "Plus, you're my favorite daughter. Mom and I would do anything for you."

"What other daughter do you have?" She squints.

I chuckle. "What do you say to burgers right now? I heard there's a place in Westwood that has some great ones. Or at least, that's what the reviews say."

"Let's find out if the reviews are right. Want to take my car or the moving van?"

"I'll drive us in the van. You can leave your car here."

I grin and rub my belly as I get into the van and fire up the engine. It's grown in size recently, I'm ashamed to say – my belly, that is. Judy and I took Annie out to eat almost every night for the last week just to treat her before going off to college. And now here we are on the campus, having just finished moving most of her possessions into her small room. It was a nice trip down here from San Francisco with Annie leading the way in her little car as I drove the moving truck. It makes me want to start bawling, to be honest, because I'm going to miss her more than anyone could ever imagine, but I manage to stop myself after letting out a single, solitary tear. Annie notices this.

"Aw, Dad. What are you crying about? I'll take trips up to San Francisco as often as I can. And you said you'll come down here to LA a lot, right?"

"All the time."

"You don't have to come *all* the time," she says, giving me a slightly worried look.

I laugh as I steer us along the road. "Just joking. But you know that Mom and I will be taking trips down here pretty often. We're going to miss our girl."

"Yeah. I'm going to miss you all too. Too bad Mom couldn't come down."

"She'd have been bawling her eyes out, so we both agreed that it's probably better she didn't. You all had your nice goodbye together this morning at the diner, anyway, while I stayed home and loaded up the van."

"Thanks for that. We both talked about how we felt kinda bad eating at the diner this morning while you were busting your butt at home getting all my stuff into this van. But you insisted. I don't know why you didn't just come with us to eat."

"Don't be silly. I insisted because I wanted you and Mom to have your time together before it was time for us to go. I know Mom needed that. Girl time, and all that."

"Thanks, Dad. Hug her for me again when you get home."

"Will do."

We make it to the burger joint after finding a parking garage, and we are seated in the middle of the restaurant by a friendly waiter wearing an old fashioned suit modeled after the ones they used to wear at greasy diners in the 1950s. It's a retro space with pictures of golden age actors and actresses on the wall, and the menu has chocolate shakes and all sorts of tasty looking desserts to wash down the burgers, hot dogs, French fries, and chicken tenders. I order a double cheeseburger with fries for myself, and Annie gets a single with some fries.

"How about a shake?" I ask.

"Oh, well, now that you mention it." She smiles.

I nod my head. "I knew you couldn't resist."

I order us two chocolate shakes and two sodas and the waiter tells us everything will be right out. Then I lean back in the booth and smile as I look around at the diner's décor.

"I like the vibe of this place. Let's see if the burgers are as good as they say."

And as if on cue, the friendly waiters strolls out a moment later with our orders, placing them directly in front of us before smiling and saying, "Enjoy your meals."

"Let's dig in," I say, smiling across the table at Annie. I'm hungry after all that loading, unloading, and hauling up steps and through narrow hallways. I'm happy to finally sit down to have lunch. Annie looks pretty happy herself, and I'm glad to see that. I want to make her happy, especially now that we are about to part ways.

"Oh, this looks super good," she says.

We both eat silently, focusing on our food until we finish every last scrap. The burger is exceptional and cooked to perfection, with fresh tomato, lettuce, pickles and cheese smashed between a deliciously toasted bun. The French fries are thin, crispy and salty, just the way I like them. As I sit enjoying the meal, I forget about pretty much everything in life except how incredible the food tastes. For the ten minutes that it takes me to finish my food, I feel like I'm experiencing some kind of a food high.

"Well, that was amazing." Annie is the first to speak as I sit there in a seemingly catatonic state with my eyes glazed over and a goofy little grin on my face. "Um, Dad. You okay?" She snaps her fingers.

I chuckle and quickly shake my head to try and snap back into the present moment. "Yeah, I'm just needing a little nap after all that tasty food," I say.

"You're not going back today, are you? That'd be crazy."

"No, I'd pass out at the wheel if I tried that." I laugh. "I booked a room in Ventura for the night. Figured I'd splurge a little and treat myself to a nice place with a jacuzzi near the beach. Your old man needs a relaxing night to himself spent doing absolutely nothing at all after all that heavy lifting he did today." I wink.

"Sounds good, Dad. And thanks again, really. Thanks so much."

"Don't thank me. I'm your old man. It's what we do."

As I drop Annie off back at her dormitory, we say our goodbyes and I do my best not to cry too much. She promises to call regularly, and I promise to visit often, and then I make my way north about an hour to the hotel in Ventura. After checking in, I plop down on the bed and lie there staring up at the ceiling, yawning. Since it's only late afternoon, I force myself to get up before I accidentally wind up falling asleep, and then I turn on the jacuzzi and have a nice hot soak before ordering room service for dinner.

After that, I lie down in bed and scroll through my phone. I'm dead tired, and plan on waking up for an early checkout and a pleasant solo drive back up the Pacific Coast Highway, but it's too early to sleep now. I think I'll just lie here for a while and rest my mind and body, then I might go out and take a little walk on the sand before coming back in and calling it a night.

I'm so glad I got Annie settled in at her dorm. I think she's going to enjoy college life, and I'm grateful the neighborhood she's in seems so safe and secure. I'm grateful Judy and I were able to have such a wonderful child. I hope she goes on to do amazing things in life, as I'm sure she will.

These last two months went by so quickly. It was a nice summer, and I wish it would have lasted a bit longer. I know that Judy and I are going to miss Annie so much, but it's for the best that she's in college and working towards her goals. We're both so happy to have raised such a fine young woman with so much strength, integrity, and intelligence.

I feel blissful as I lie here in bed, thinking about how fortunate we are.

But suddenly I remember how just two months ago things seemed so frightening for several days, with the horrible young man from New York showing up and trying to worm his way back into our lives. The darkness I felt during those days was in stark contrast to the warmth I feel now. Thank goodness that all ended quickly.

I wonder what happened to him. I guess he felt embarrassed after that last encounter outside our house, and seeing that we wanted nothing to do with him or his apology, he simply left town. That's what Lieutenant Morton seemed to think, anyway.

Well, it doesn't really matter at this point, and there is no use in pondering over it too much. He's gone now – back to New York, I'd say – and my wife and daughter are safe. That's all that matters in the end.

Annie and Judy are safe.

Chapter Twenty-Five
Annie

I hope Dad gets a good night's sleep before driving back to San Francisco tomorrow. I'm really grateful that he helped move all my things down here. My roommate is really nice, which I'm thankful for, because I was worried about sharing living quarters with someone who ended up being rude or weird. Fortunately, she is neither, and even though it's been a busy day, we still managed to find some time to go out for coffee and cake at a nearby café. I'm excited for classes tomorrow, and I'm wondering how they will go.

Suffice to say, I'm having a blast so far, and I bet once things settle down, I'll be having even more fun.

It's about nine o'clock at night now and I feel like I need to move around a bit. I know I should start winding down and go to sleep soon, but I feel wired. I guess it's the excitement of being in a new city and starting a new chapter in life. I think I'll go for a walk. I still haven't walked around outside of campus yet. It would be nice to go out and see the city a bit. I know LA isn't known for being a walkable city, by any means, but I don't feel like driving right now. I'd like to just get out and stretch my legs a bit. I'd invite my roommate, but she isn't home right now, so that means it'll be just me, which I don't mind – it gives me time to think and plan for my future. I like to set goals when I'm out taking walks, and I think tonight will be the perfect time to set several.

The sun has set and taken the warmth of the day along with it. It's turned into a chilly night, but the crisp air feels good on my skin as I stroll out past the edge of campus and onto Wilshire Boulevard. While it feels fun to explore the area, there doesn't seem to be a whole lot around here. For the most part, I seem to be mostly passing tall apartment complexes. I guess this area of town is mostly residential. To see a bit of urban hustle and bustle, I think I'd have to walk east pretty far, and I don't know if I have enough energy (or time) for that tonight. Class comes early tomorrow. And besides, I'm not walking around to sightsee, I'm here to plan.

But just as I begin thinking about my plans for what I'll do upon graduating in four years, I hear a deep voice call out from close behind me.

"Excuse me, ma'am, you wouldn't happen to be Annie, would you?"

It's a voice that isn't entirely familiar, and yet I seem to recognize it. The accent isn't from here. It's Northeastern – New York, from what it sounds like. And the realization of that makes a chill trickle down the nape of my neck as I spin around quickly and face whoever the voice belongs to.

I just pray it doesn't belong to *him*, although I know it must. Who else would it be?

Sure enough, there he stands, with his hands in the pockets of his blue jeans and a dingy, scuffed looking leather jacket draped over his bulging, weightlifter physique. He is wearing an old, sweat-stained ball cap and his eyes are obscured by the darkness beneath the bill. But there is no mistaking the visible lower half of his face, nor is there any mistaking the size of him. It was the first thing I'd noticed upon seeing him in San Francisco two months ago – he had grown immensely in the last seven years.

Before I can scream, he holds a hand up and gives me a nervous glance. "I swear, this is just a crazy coincidence – us running into each other, I mean. I got a job down here in LA with a company that helps reform ex-cons. It's low paying temporary work, but they offered me a place to stay in a rooming house and-"

"Sorry, I have to get going," I say shakily, trying to stand my ground and sound strong. Trying, but probably not succeeding. I'm nervous, and there is no hiding that.

Because he's lying to me. This can't be a coincidence. No. That's too far-fetched. It's simply unbelievable that he would have gotten a job *here* in this area at the same time I began attending college here. He's lying about everything.

"Okay, but please just understand that this is a wild coincidence." He smiles awkwardly as he peers at me with an anxious look on his face. "This is just as uncomfortable for me as it is for you. Believe me, after your dad beat me up, the last thing I'd want to do is make him upset again. That was humiliating."

"I've really got to go," I say, glancing across the wide road for oncoming traffic. No cars are approaching in either direction, and there are no other pedestrians that I can see. It's just the two of us, all alone in this quiet neighborhood.

I nervously rush across the road, looking behind me repeatedly until I make it to the other side. But Tony doesn't follow me. He just stands there with his hands in his pockets, gazing at me. Slowly he pulls a hand from his pocket and waves it at me.

I turn and start to jog. The jog quickly turns into a full-fledged sprint.

By the time I make it back to my dorm and slam the door shut behind me, I'm dripping sweat.

Please don't let this nightmare be starting up again. Not here. Not now.

Chapter Twenty-Six
Bruce

    After dinner I take a little stroll on the sand and stare out at the Pacific for a while, just sitting there on the beach with my hands over my knees, thinking about life and all its strange mysteries. I'm glad I booked this hotel instead of getting the cheaper option further inland. It's only going to be one night, but it's going to be a nice, relaxing night. I even brought a novel with me to read for a while before I pass out. I'm sure that won't take long. Even now as I walk barefoot through the sand with the cold tide rolling in at my feet, I feel exhausted.

    It's about nine o'clock, or thereabouts. I stop walking for a moment and turn to face the water as the bubbly white tide rolls in at my feet and dances up around my ankles for a moment before being drawn back out to sea. It's a beautiful world, that's for sure. Even if I never figure out the meaning of life and all its mysteries, at least I can admit that – nature sure is beautiful. Maybe that's all there is to know. Maybe there are no answers to any of the age old questions. Maybe –

    Suddenly, my phone rings in my pocket, stirring me out of my deep thinking. I pull it out, look down at the screen, and feel a twinge of anxiety come over me when I see Annie's name. Maybe she just wants to chat. Maybe she's just got a question about something. She's living on her own for the first time, so I'm sure she'll be calling me to ask little questions about things from time to time. I quickly put the phone to my ear.

"Hi, Annie, is everything okay?"

The sound of her breathing answers my question before her voice can. She sounds out of breath and distressed. "Annie?" I say.

"Dad," she says quickly. "I just saw the guy. Tony. I just saw him down on Wilshire Boulevard."

"What? Oh my God," I stammer, feeling flushed as I spin in circles on the sand, trying to comprehend what she just said. "Okay, where are you? Are you home?"

"Yes."

"Is your door locked? Are you with your roommate, Jaylyn?"

"She's not home – I've got the door locked, Dad." Her breathing calms down a little. Her voice seems to become a bit less shaky.

I take a breath and try to make sense of it.

"What happened?" I murmur, feeling a dizzy sense of confusion take hold of me.

I don't understand how this can be happening right now.

"I just went on a walk. It was on Wilshire Boulevard, which is just down from my dorm. I was walking alone when I heard him call out behind me. I turned and he tried to play it off like it was a coincidence."

"Like hell it's a coincidence," I shout, then wince at my own voice and shake my head. "Sorry, honey. Sorry for yelling, I'm just worked up now. I can't believe this."

Annie continues: "He said he got some kind of job or something with a company that helps reform ex-prisoners. Something like that. He said they'd given him a place to stay. I don't know, Dad. It was so shocking. I felt like my heart stopped for a second."

"God, I can't blame you. He's the last person you'd expect to see. But you're okay now. That's what matters." I pause, trying to catch my breath. "What happened then?"

She tells me everything. I stand there on the sand digging my toes into it, clenching them nervously as I lick my lips anxiously and feel my eyes shifting all around me. I can't seem to calm down. This doesn't feel real.

Why is this creep still in California? Why hasn't he been arrested and locked up yet?

"Annie, I'm going to come to your dorm now. We'll figure this out. I'm sorry this is happening, but listen, don't worry, okay? We'll get this figured out. I'm going to call Bill Morton now to see if he can get ahold of some people in the LAPD. I'm sure he'll know what to do. Maybe he can make some phone calls and they can find out where this creep is staying. But listen, just keep your doors locked, okay? I'll be there soon. Leaving in ten."

"I already called the cops. That was the first thing I did when I got home. They said they'd send someone over to get a statement from me."

"Oh." I breathe a sweet sigh of relief and smile softly. She's smart. Always was. That was the right move, calling them immediately. "That's perfect. I'll still try to get ahold of Bill to see if he can escalate the situation. Now just stay put, and I'll be there as soon as I can."

"Drive carefully, Dad. I'm okay now. Don't get into a wreck or anything stupid."

"I know. I'll be okay."

I put my phone back in my pocket and stare out at the ocean for a few seconds as I try to calm down, but it's useless. All the breathing exercises in the world and meditation techniques couldn't help me now. I know I won't be able to relax until I'm with Annie. I turn around and start running towards the hotel parking lot as my heart ricochets in my chest like a basketball being slammed repeatedly against the pavement.

I don't believe this. Any of it.

And there is no way this is a coincidence.

He *followed* us down to Southern California, didn't he? He must have. But why? What does he *want*? Why is he *doing* this?

Does he blame Judy and me for his brother's death? And for the two of them getting caught in the first place? Does he just want to toy with me by taunting my family, pretending to be some nice, reformed kidnapper? Is that what the sick freak wants? To psychologically torture us?

When I reach the rental van, I jerk the door open and hop up into the seat. Then, jamming the key into the ignition, I slam my foot on the gas pedal as I reverse out of the parking space. My hand instinctively thrusts the gear shifter into drive, and I pound my foot once more on the gas, hightailing it south down the freeway towards Los Angeles. I catch myself trembling in the rearview mirror as I steer the wheel, and a cold sweat drips relentlessly down my face and neck. I look like I've seen a ghost.

    I need to get there as quickly as possible.

    I need to figure this out and get this creep away from my daughter.

    And I won't leave LA until that happens.

Chapter Twenty-Seven
Judy

I almost choke on my water when I hear what Annie has just told me.

"What? Honey, tell me you're kidding."

But she isn't kidding. I wish more than anything that she was, but I know she's not the type who would ever kid about something as serious as this. She wouldn't want her father or me to have a heart attack over a cruel joke like that.

She says nothing, and the silence speaks volumes. She's scared. I can't blame her. I'm scared *for* her and I'm all the way up here in Northern California. That makes me feel even worse as far as being scared goes, really, because I know I can't do anything to help from this far away. I feel useless. This was supposed to be the start of something wonderful for our girl.

"You called the police, right?"

"Yeah. That was the first thing I did. I know some people might say it was an overreaction, but-"

"No," I cut her off. "It was absolutely *not* an overreaction to call them. It would be foolish not to."

I want to give her some words of encouragement, but what can I say? I feel hopeless right now, to say the very least – not to mention caught entirely off guard by this news. I can't believe it. He showed up down there? All the way down in Los Angeles? He's truly stalking her now, isn't he?

He's stalking our daughter and he's not going to stop until he's put away again.

For whatever reason, he can't seem to let this go.

"Mom, are you okay?"

"Of course, honey." I try to sound strong, but even *I* am aware of the trembling in my voice.

"I can tell you're upset. Please don't worry. I'm sure everything will be fine; I just knew I needed to tell you what happened."

She's right, of course. I'm upset, but everything will be fine. It'll work out soon.

Won't it?

I'm just overwhelmed after hearing this. I catch myself gulping repeatedly. Whenever I'm under any kind of severe stress, I always feel like my body starts working overtime – rapid heartbeat, excess saliva, sweat dripping from every inch of my skin, shakiness, lightheadedness. Although I guess that's not unique to me. I'm not special in that regard. In fact I'd say most people react similarly to stress, although I may react more intensely than some. Bruce is the same. I'm sure he's feeling just as worked up as I am right now.

"Annie, is your father there yet?"

"No. The cops aren't here either. I guess they'll be here soon."

"Okay. Keep your doors locked until they get there. I'm going to call your father now, okay?"

"Okay. But Mom, please don't get worked up over this – either of you. Don't worry. I don't want to make you all stressed. When you're stressed, I'm stressed."

"I know, sweetie," I say, trying to laugh a little to lighten the mood. "I promise you that I'll try my hardest, okay? And I promise I won't get Dad worked up on the phone. I'll talk to you soon, okay?"

"Okay. Love you."

"Love you too, Annie."

I take a breath before clicking Bruce's name. He answers quickly.

"Honey?" He says.

"Annie just told me. Are you close to the campus?"

"Yeah. I'll be there in about fifteen minutes, give or take. Don't worry. This guy's going to get nabbed. He's trying to play it off as a coincidence. That's a load of nonsense, to say the least."

"I know. He's lying to her. And he probably knows that she knows it's a lie."

"He's messing with us. That's what he's doing. He's trying to get under our skin. I just got off the phone with Bill Morton. He said he'd see what he could do about reaching out to the LAPD. Surprisingly, he doesn't know too many people down here, but maybe he'll still be able to help pull some strings anyhow. I don't know, though."

"Just get there soon and talk to the police. Annie says they haven't gotten there yet, so maybe you'll arrive around the same time. You must be tired from all the driving."

"No, I'm feeling pretty hyped up. It's the adrenaline, I guess."

"Well, don't get too stressed, please, Bruce."

"Honey, I won't be able to let myself leave LA until this is over. I don't care if that makes me sound like an overbearing parent. This guy kidnapped our daughter seven years ago and now the creep is stalking her right after getting released from prison."

"You don't have to convince me, Bruce. We're on the same page."

"Good," he sighs, adding. "I guess I'll drive back to Ventura tonight and sleep after talking to the police. It's not so far from LA, especially when traffic is light at night. Tomorrow I'll book a room in the city. Something close to Annie."

"I'll come down, too, if this doesn't get sorted out within the next day or two."

"Oh, you don't have to," he says, but I know he wants me to. I can hear it in the tone of his voice.

"I will."

"Okay. I'll keep you updated. But you should get some sleep now, okay? You've got clients tomorrow, right?"

"Yeah, I've got six."

"Busy day. Just don't worry, okay?"

"I should be the one telling you that, Bruce."

"I'm okay," he says. "I love you, Judy."

"I love you too. Call me later and tell me what the police say. Just give me an update, okay? Even if it's late. I don't care."

"I will."

I sit brooding at the dinner table, staring out at the dark street as I sip my water and think about how everything has become so incredibly chaotic all of a sudden. For two months I hardly even thought of that man, and when I *did* think of him, they were pleasant thoughts about how happy I was that it was over; that he'd gone home and left us alone. Now I feel so naïve, and I wonder when it will truly be over. I hope it will be soon. I hope there will be some sort of closure in the next few days.

A chilling thought comes over me.

What if the police aren't able to locate him, and what if Annie simply doesn't see him again? What if there *is* no closure, and it's constantly eating at us in the back of our minds as we wait and wonder if he will pop up again at random? That's what scares me the most, I think – the possibility that he'll just vanish and reappear when Annie least expects it, when her guard is down the most.

It's a nightmarish thought for a parent to have, especially with Annie being so far away from me, living on her own in a new city for the first time in her life.

I don't know what I can do. If the police can't find the man, what then? What will happen next?

They'll be able to find him, I tell myself, silently repeating it as I try to lull myself into a sense of hopefulness.

But the truth is that I'm frightened of what might happen – deathly frightened.

I have no idea what will happen next.

Chapter Twenty-Eight
Annie

There is a knock on the door. "Police, ma'am," a calm voice says.

I stand up and seem to levitate towards the door. My legs feel like noodles right now. Not just from all the running, but also from my blood pressure spiking, I guess. I open the door and see two officers standing together, a woman and a man.

"Hello, I'm Officer Hartwell," the woman says. "You reported a man following you?"

"Yes, you can come in if you'd like. Sorry, it's kind of a cramped little room."

"That's quite alright," the man says as he steps into the room with the other following.

They glance around at the walls for a brief moment before looking back at me. I suppose they are waiting for me to get on with whatever it is I have to tell them. It's been a long time since I talked to police officers before, and I feel all those memories from seven years ago rushing back into my mind. I wish I could block those awful memories out of my mind, but I know I can't. Not with him creeping around nearby.

"Well, I think he was following me," I say. "I'm ninety-nine percent sure he was. He claims it was a coincidence, the two of us running into each other, but I know that would be pretty much impossible."

"And why's that, ma'am?" The male cop wears a nametag that reads Bryant. He stares at me with a scrunched brow.

I begin the process of telling the entire story, starting back in New York seven years ago when I was kidnapped. Then I wrap up the story with what happened less than an hour ago. It doesn't take long, but the story still feels so intense when I tell it, and it honestly feels pretty surreal to be here in this position, seven years and three thousand miles away from New York City but still going up against the same sick individual. I stay strong, however, and I don't cry.

"That's a heck of a story. I'm glad you're okay." Officer Hartwell shakes her head and stares down at her notepad before looking at me again. "Can you give us a detailed description of the suspect, as well as his full name?"

Just then, Dad barges through the door. For a moment, I feel like the cops are caught off guard by this random man suddenly appearing, and I'm frightened that they're going to reach for their guns or something crazy like in a movie, but thankfully Dad quickly gets rid of any worries they have when he says, "Oh, thank goodness you're here. I'm Bruce Hurt, Annie's father. I came as soon as she told me."

Dad being here takes a big load off of me. I don't have to go through all the details myself. Instead I just sit around and listen as he tells the police all the information we know about Tony. It isn't much, really, but at least Dad knows his last name and some details about the court case. He also mentions that the man's brother was killed while in prison and brings up the possibility of that being the reason Tony showed up here. Maybe he wants revenge.

I tune a lot of it out, to be honest. None of it is important to me, and I don't like hearing about this man or even thinking about him. Still, I know I can't ignore it entirely, because he's here, and until they manage to find him, I suspect he's here to stay.

I don't like that, but that's the reality I've found myself in, and until that reality changes, I guess I'm stuck in it.

My roommate Jaylyn comes home and everyone turns their head. She almost jumps when she opens the door and sees us all standing there. "What happened?" She gasps.

I tell her the situation, trying to make it seem like it is not that big of a deal, but I can tell she still seems more than a little freaked out. I can't blame her, but it really is unfortunate, because now I worry she might harbor bad feelings towards me for being her roommate. I hope she doesn't feel like I'm putting her at any sort of risk, because I'd never want that to be the case, and up until tonight, I didn't even think that it was a possibility. But now? Now all bets are off. What if he comes after her as well? Simply for being around me.

The cops stick around for quite a bit longer than I thought they would. They're very thorough. It's a good thing, despite the fact that I'm sure Jaylyn is feeling overwhelmed by their presence, and also the fact that I've got classes early in the morning. That doesn't matter in the grand scheme of things, though. I'd rather us be inconvenienced and a little uncomfortable by them sticking around and doing a thorough job instead of them brushing it off and acting bored. I'm glad that these cops seem to be interested in doing their jobs as best as they can. They actually seem like they want to help.

I hope they're able to.

"Alright, folks, I think that about wraps things up," Officer Hartwell closes her notebook and says something into her radio that sounds like cop jargon to me. She puts the radio back on her hip and smiles at me. "We've got his name now, so we're hoping they'll be able to find an address and place of employment. If what he's telling you is true about him being employed, it shouldn't take too long."

And what if he's lying?

I nod my head and smile at them both. "Thank you for your help."

They say goodbye to us and leave.

Now it's just Dad and Jaylyn and me. He stands there awkwardly and then goes over to the window to peer out through the blinds. He's very on edge, I can tell. Jaylyn sits on her bed and doesn't say anything. She looks weirded out by everything that's happened. I'm sure if I were in her shoes, I'd be feeling the same. I hope I'll be able to reassure her later that she's not in any danger.

But am I really sure of that myself?

"It's okay, Dad." I stand by him at the window. He turns quickly, his frowning lips twitching anxiously, and then he forces a little smile at me.

"Yeah," he says softly. "Yeah, it'll be okay. I'm going to stay in Ventura tonight and then tomorrow I'll be coming back down to LA. I'll stick around here for a while until the dust settles. We're going to get this sorted out, so don't you worry." He looks at Jaylyn and smiles again as he waves a hand awkwardly. "I promise our lives aren't normally so chaotic. It's just this one little problem that's been badgering us lately. But I'm sure it'll be over soon."

Jaylyn gives him a worried looking half-smile and nods but doesn't say anything.

Dad turns and looks out the window again. I want to tell him he doesn't have to stay in town, and that I'll be fine on my own, and that the police will handle it – but I don't. Because I know it would be no use. Dad, being as worried as he is, is not going to take no for an answer when it comes to watching out for me. The experience in New York changed him, I guess. It changed all of us.

I know he won't bug me or be annoying about it. He knows I'm here to study and learn. He's not crazily protective, by any means. But I know he will be sticking close by, probably staying at a hotel on the outskirts of campus, waiting and watching. I don't think he needs to do that, but if it makes him feel better, then I don't mind. He's my dad, after all, and I know he worries about me.

Before leaving, he gives me a big hug and tells me that everything will be okay. I can tell he is just saying this to make me feel better. Deep down, he is worried that things *won't* be okay.

I'm worried about that, too.

Chapter Twenty-Nine
Bruce

I drive back to the hotel in Ventura feeling a little better about things, but I'm still shaken up by all that's happened. It would be one thing if I had expected it as a possibility, but the thought of him showing up here in Southern California never crossed my mind. God, how silly was I to think that it was all over. Although I guess I can't blame myself too much, because it did seem like it was over. I never thought my family would lay eyes on him again, not after that night two months ago in front of our house.

I thought he was gone after that. So now this means he *was* lying about wanting to apologize – not that I believed his whole spiel about that in the first place, anyway. He must have come out here to California for some other vengeful reason. It makes my skin feel like it's crawling when I try to think about his agenda. He spent about seven years locked away, and now he's out and the first thing he does is come here to bother my family.

And I don't think that *bothering* us is all he wants to do. That is just the tip of the iceberg. I know I may be sounding paranoid, but I'm terrified that this man wants blood. But we can't prove that. All the cops will be able to do, I guess, is arrest him for violating his parole when – *if* – they find him. And that's a big if. They might not find him, and even if they do, I'm not sure of what kind of charges he'd get.

I wish I were well versed in law, but that's never been my area of expertise.

I've got so much on my mind as I drive north on the dark highway. I feel both exhausted and frazzled, as if I just decided to drink three cups of coffee a moment before lying down to go to bed. It's a bad feeling, and I hope I manage to get some quality sleep tonight, because I know I'll need the energy tomorrow. I plan on going back down to Los Angeles, checking into a hotel, and then going out and walking the streets. It probably seems a bit over the top, but I'm hoping I'll be able to get a sight of him. It's a big city, so I doubt that'll happen. But I've got to try.

But then again, what if I *do* see him? What would I even do about it?

I'm not going to take the law into my own hands. I know I threatened him back in San Francisco and even beat him up pretty good. But he let me do that, and in reality I'm not some sort of tough guy vigilante, and he knows that. It pains me to admit this, but I probably wouldn't stand a chance against him if he decided to put up a fight.

So I have no choice but to settle this non-violently. In fact, I probably won't even approach him. I know it will be hard to resist, because I want to give him a strong-worded piece of my mind, but it'll be the best course of action. If I *do* end up seeing him on the streets, what I think I'll do is try to stay hidden while I follow him and call the police. I'll stay on the line with the dispatcher while they send someone to my location. Hopefully I won't lose him. I'll try to follow him wherever he's going. But this is all assuming that the cops don't locate him before I start trying to. For all I know, they might be able to find the creep tonight. But I'm not holding my breath.

After pulling into the hotel garage, I sit in the moving van and stare out at the night sky. It's a big world out there. Why'd he have to come all the way here from New York? Why did he have to come and torment us again? It's not our fault he broke the law by kidnapping our daughter and demanding a ransom. It's not our fault he got sentenced to prison along with his brother. And it's not our fault his brother got killed while in prison.

None of it is our fault. He was the one who made the choice to take our sweet Annie, and now he's blaming us for the repercussions of his actions. It's all so infuriating and nonsensical, but I guess he has somehow rationalized it to himself. He's somehow talked himself into believing that it's *our* fault, and that he deserves revenge. I guess those years spent locked up did a number on him mentally, but then again, considering he was already willing to commit kidnapping as a juvenile, I suspect he might have been a bit nuts to begin with.

Or simply evil.

And here I go again, trying to analyze the situation. It's silly. I'm making myself feel frustrated. I should just take a deep breath and admit that there is no use in trying to figure out his motives. He's here, and he's clearly a threat to Annie, and that's the only thing that matters.

He has to be found and stopped.

A while later, I lie in bed and close my eyes. I toss and turn for what feels like an eternity, but after a while, I manage to fall asleep. Then the dreams come.

I see her walking along the Santa Monica Pier. She's the only one there. The sky is baby blue and cloudless. She's smiling as she stares at the sights. Then the sky turns dark gray as if a violent storm is about to roll in. A moment later a shadow approaches her from behind. It is a man wearing a long, dark trenchcoat.

It is Tony.

A sick smile curls up at the edges of his lips as a blade appears in his hand. It glimmers as he holds it up in the air and lets out a howling scream. Then he takes off running towards Annie, who has nowhere to go. She runs, screaming, towards the end of the pier.

There is nowhere to go. It's a dead end. The only way out is to jump into the sea. And what if he jumps in right after her?

I wake up gasping and clutching my stomach. I feel sick. I run my hand up along my sweat-soaked torso to my face, which is also drenched. It was just a dream. A twisted, demented, horrifying dream. But that's all it was. A dream. A nightmare. It wasn't real.

"…Just a dream," I murmur, standing up from bed and walking on shaky legs towards the bathroom. I stare at my reflection in the mirror and feel dazed as I hardly recognize the man looking back at me. Dark, puffy bags sit beneath bloodshot eyes. I look like I didn't get a wink of sleep, and my mouth feels like I swallowed a bag of sand.

I check my watch and see that it's just five. It's too early to make my way down towards LA. What I need to do now is sleep. I'll need the energy. If I don't sleep, I'll feel even more frantic than I already do, and that won't help me sort this mess out. I've got to be rested and levelheaded, or else I'll get nowhere.

I pour some water into a paper cup and down it in one gulp, then repeat this several times. Then I wipe the sweat from my chest with a damp towel before crawling back into bed and closing my eyes. Sleep comes quickly, and thankfully the bad dreams don't come along with it.

When I wake up to the sound of my alarm blaring, it is seven o'clock and time for me to shower and head back to Los Angeles.

Chapter Thirty
Judy

Despite both Bruce and Annie telling me the situation, I can't seem to shake the feeling that I'm in the dark up here in San Francisco. It's not any fault of theirs, of course, as they have told me all there is to know. It's just the simple fact that I'm so far away. I think I might consider taking a flight down there tonight once I finish work today. I could cancel my training sessions for tomorrow and reschedule. I've been working with most of these clients for so long - they'll understand. And if they didn't, so what? My daughter comes first, and while I'm glad Bruce is involved in helping out down there, I know I need to be involved as well.

Although I don't want to do anything that makes Annie feel more stressed.

My phone rings as I fix my morning eggs and coffee. It's Bruce.

"Hi. How's it going?" I ask.

"I've got you on speaker. I'm driving to LA now. Traffic is all backed up on the freeway, but I'll get there sooner or later. Did you sleep well?"

"I slept okay. What about you?"

"Not at first. Had weird dreams. Oh well. They were just dreams. What time's your first client?"

"Nine fifteen. I was thinking tonight I might fly down to LA. What do you think?"

He hesitates for a moment. "I think that'd be good, but let's talk with Annie about it. I'd be lying if I said it wouldn't be nice having you around for a while. I miss you. And I'm sure Annie misses you too already."

"Aw, I'd say she's had enough of the two of us for a while, but that's a sweet thought. And I miss you too. Both of you. I want to be there while this is going on. I just feel so overwhelmed when I think about it."

"You and I both. Part of being a parent, I guess. We're worried about our little girl, even though she's not so little anymore. I guess that worrying will never stop." He chuckles softly.

"Especially not with this guy roaming around. I don't get it. I really don't get it, Bruce. Did he follow you all down from San Francisco, do you think?"

He sighs and doesn't say anything for a moment. It's as if he is thinking it over. Then he finally speaks. "He pretty much had to have, I think. But I don't know. I'd been thinking about that before I called you. I figure he probably did exactly that. But that means he probably never left San Francisco to begin with. God knows what the creep's been doing for two months. Or maybe I'm wrong about that. I have no idea. I don't know where he's been or what he's been up to these last two months, but he had to have known somehow that we were heading down to LA when we did, and he had to have followed us. This nonsense he spouted off about it being a coincidence is just that: nonsense. He didn't get a job down here. That's a lie. You and I both know that." He pauses, taking a shaky breath, then adds, "Maybe he'd been sticking around in San Francisco somehow.

I don't know where he'd be staying or how he could afford it for two months. But maybe he saw us renting the moving van and followed us."

"We don't know that he didn't have some sort of money when he went to prison. He'd get that back afterwards, I guess," I say.

"Yeah, there's that possibility. Or he could have stolen money. Who knows. We really don't know much about this guy at all, do we? We just know he was a punk who took part in kidnapping Annie. I never was interested in learning anything else about the guy. I don't want to know his life story because he makes me sick. But I'm wondering how he's doing this, and why? But I guess the why is simple enough. He hates us. Wants revenge. Thinks we owe it to him. He was a kid when he went to jail; he couldn't have had much money in his bank account. Either way, he's causing us trouble, and I'm ready to fix it."

"What's that mean? Don't do anything stupid, Bruce. Please."

"You know I don't mean anything like that. I'm not going to try to hurt the guy. I'm just going to work with the cops and make sure they're doing everything they can to put a stop to this. I'll make sure they're not monkeying around. Our daughter's life could be at stake."

"Don't say that," I tell him softly, but I know he's right. It just isn't something I want to hear.

He stays quiet on the other end. I sit there sipping my coffee and staring down at my eggs. I'm not that hungry now, but I'll make myself eat at least a little. It could end up being a long day if I choose to fly down to LA tonight, and I know I can't get by on an empty stomach.

"She's going to be okay," Bruce says. "I'll keep you informed on what's going on, okay? Let's all do a little video call later."

"Okay," I say.

"I love you, Judy."

"I love you too."

Chapter Thirty-One
Annie

It's about six o'clock when I wake up without an alarm despite going to bed pretty late last night. I slept pretty good, even if it wasn't enough. I had weird dreams, though. Unsurprisingly, they were about *him*. And unlike a lot of dreams, I remember them vividly. I remember I was lying on a bed in the middle of some room with dark walls. The foot of the bed was facing a door. It wasn't my room – I've never had a room look like that.

I couldn't move from the bed. I remember lying there feeling like my entire body was numb, like when you sleep on your arm a funny way and it feels dead. My whole body felt like it had pins and needles digging into it. Then there was another knock, followed by the sound of a squeaky doorknob being twisted.

Slowly it opened. A sense of dread began to waft in through the cracked door like heat rising from a furnace. The room was incredibly quiet. Then a hand holding a bouquet of roses quickly slipped through the crack.

A shy, muffled voice spoke from behind the door. "It's me. Can I come in? I got you these. See? I know it's not much, but I just wanted to get you something nice, just to show you that I'm sorry. I picked them out at a flower shop nearby. I can come back tomorrow with more if you'd like. They had all sorts of flowers. I might go get some for your parents, too. Everybody likes flowers, don't they? I wish they'd give me a chance. Your parents, I mean. Can I come in? I just want to talk. It's really a coincidence, me being here in town, and I want you to understand that. I also want you to understand how sorry I am. I changed a lot inside, I'm not lying about that, and if I could just earn your trust and forgiveness it would mean the world to me. It would bring me a lot of peace. Could you help me earn that? Tell me what to do and I'll do it. I want to make things right between us, between me, you, and your folks. Now how about we sit down and talk it over? You're starting to make me a little upset."

    I woke up right after that with my heart pounding.

    And now here I lie gazing up at the ceiling. *It was just a stupid dream,* I tell myself. When I finally decide to get up and crawl out of bed, Jaylyn is still snoring across the room. I quietly tiptoe over to the window where the couch is and then sit down and start looking over some reading material for one of my classes. Jaylyn stirs and starts to snore a little after rolling onto her back. A few minutes later her alarm begins blaring, and she jumps upright and murmurs sleepily, "I'm up. I'm up."

    She turns and gives me a weary looking yawn. "Morning," she says.

    "Morning." I smile. "Sleep good?"

"Yeah. I could use another hour though. Or maybe three." She laughs and pushes herself out of the bed.

She gets ready a while later and heads out before I do. I sit there on the couch and read for a while longer before I gather my belongings and stuff them into my backpack. Time has passed so quickly this morning, and I've hardly thought about the creep from last night. I hope the police will handle it. I know that Dad is coming down sometime today, and I hope he doesn't get too stressed about it all. I can always tell when he's stressed – his face and neck get so red. I don't want his blood pressure to rise over this idiot who's decided to come down to Los Angeles and stalk me.

Not that I don't take it seriously. I *do*. I know that this Tony guy is a threat, but I'm eighteen now, and that's a far cry from being eleven, so in many ways I'm able to take care of myself much more than I was back then. Would I be able to fight him off if he attacked me? Probably not, but I'm almost certain it won't come to that. With Dad coming down here to keep an eye out, and the police supposedly looking for this guy, I think it'll all be over pretty quickly.

The day starts out nice. I go to class, come home during the break, head to the next class, and then move on to the next. I check my phone briefly between each class, but Dad hasn't sent me any texts. I'm guessing he doesn't want to make a big deal out of this thing, even though I know it's a big deal to him. I'm sure he's somewhere nearby now, probably checked into the closest hotel he could possibly find. He's a good dad, and I hope that this is over soon not just for my sake, but also for his, and of course for my mom's sake as well.

After my last class, I check my phone again and see that Dad has finally messaged me. It reads: *Hey, kiddo. Got a room in Santa Monica about twenty minutes from where you are, give or take a few depending on traffic. Closest place I could find. Looked in Westwood but there weren't any available options. Give me a shout when you finish class for the day. I'd like to take you out for a bite to eat unless you've got plans otherwise. Talk soon, Dad.*

I call him and he answers after the first ring. "Hi, kiddo. How were your classes?" He sounds relaxed, as if Tony isn't even on his mind. But I'm sure that he's been thinking about him all day long. He dwells on things like that, and I can't blame him.

"They were great. How's the hotel?"

"It's just a basic place. Nothing fancy. But it's clean and has a bed to sleep on, so that's all I need. I didn't hear much from the police today. I tried to call and check in but didn't get much information. Want to meet up for dinner?"

"Yeah, sure. Where?"

"I'll swing by and pick you up. You want me to come now?"

"Yeah, okay. I'm not too hungry, but I'm getting there. And with LA traffic being the way it is, I'm sure I'll be hungry by the time we get to wherever it is we're going."

He chuckles. "Yeah. I figured we'd find a place near you to eat. We'll drive around and find something, or you can look on your phone and check to see if there's any restaurant you'd like to go to. I'll just put my shoes on and head your way. See ya soon."

"Thanks, Dad. See you. Drive safe."

About an hour later we arrive at an Italian restaurant near Century City. Dad and I sit at a cozy booth with red, cushy leather. The lighting is dim and I feel relaxed in here. Dad sighs and cracks his neck slowly from side to side.

"Long day?" I ask.

"Not really. Just haven't had to drive this much in a while." He smiles.

"Thanks, Dad. For everything, I mean."

He makes a dismissive face and waves his hand. "It's nothing. I'm just being a parent. Thank *you* for not being annoyed with me." He laughs.

"Why would I be annoyed?"

He flips through the menu for a moment before looking up at me, then shrugs. "I guess there could be an argument made that I'm being overprotective. But I'm just worried about you, and I'd like to think that most parents would be doing the same thing I'm doing; sticking close until the danger is dealt with."

I shake my head and chuckle. "No, I get it. And I appreciate it. I don't want you to think I'm annoyed by it because I'm not. It's not like it's some farfetched, silly little thing that you're worried about. I'm worried, too. I don't like him being here anymore than you do – the guy *kidnapped* me." I pause and close my eyes. I don't even like saying those words. It's so uncomfortable for me to even say it out loud. But it's reality, and I'm not going to deny what happened just because it makes me feel uncomfortable. I don't want to sugarcoat things. Dad and Mom have every reason to be worried, and so do I.

I just hope it turns out that we're worrying over nothing, though.

"I'm sorry you're going through this during your first week at school. But listen, honey, it'll be sorted out soon."

I smile at him. He smiles back and then we look down at our menus and decide. The waiter comes and takes our orders, and we talk about light things for a while, and Dad of course asks me a lot about my classes. He mentions that Mom might come down to LA, but I tell him I don't think she needs to do that right away.

"She's got work. You can take off, but she's got clients she'd have to cancel on."

"She might've already rescheduled them. I haven't talked to her since this morning."

"Tell her she doesn't have to come just yet. Surely this will be finished soon. I mean, I don't see any reason we need to have the whole family down here. I don't want everything to be disrupted by this creep."

"Okay. I understand that. But you know she might still come, right?" He smiles, adding, "She's worried about you just as much as I am. You're still our little girl."

I grin and nod my head. "I know. I bet she'll still insist on coming down here. Well, that's okay, I guess. But really, I'd rather she doesn't upend her work week over this."

A moment later the waiter brings out our food – and what lovely food it appears to be. Spaghetti with meatballs, brick oven pizza, and a big, massive lasagna. The smell is heavenly, and I close my eyes and grin as I take it all in. We dig in and enjoy our food, and neither of us talk about Tony again, at least for the time being. I like it that way. I don't want him to be at the forefront of my mind all the time because I know worrying will get me nowhere.

And besides, I'm sure the police will call contact us soon enough and let us know they've located him, and then they'll reassure me that I can rest easy now and go about my way without worrying about being stalked.

I'm sure that'll happen.

Or is that just wishful thinking on my part?

Chapter Thirty-Two
Judy

Just as I'm preparing to call my next few days' worth of clients to reschedule, my phone begins to ring. It's Bruce.

"Hey, hon. Sorry, I don't know if I'll be able to make the night flight tonight, but I'll be on the first plane coming down tomorrow. I was just about to start rescheduling with my clients."

"Oh, that's why I was calling, hon. I'm here with Annie. Want to say hi?" He turns on his video, and I see the two of them flashing smiles and waving at me. "We're sitting here in the van outside a restaurant. We just had Italian for dinner."

"Hi, Mom," Annie says.

"Hi, honey. Aw, it's so good to see you two smiling. I know it hasn't been all that long since you guys left, but it feels like it's been ages."

"I know. It's been crazy. But Mom, I was telling Dad I think that this is going to be over soon. I mean, I think it'd be silly for you to have to reschedule all these people, you know what I mean? I've already disrupted Dad's work, and now I'm disrupting yours."

"Honey, I don't mind, and neither would my clients," I say, adding, "And you'd better believe I'm coming down."

"It's just that I'd rather have you both down here to celebrate something fun, like this annoying problem being solved. How about you wait until the cops find the guy, then we can all have a relaxing time together down here in LA? That would be more fun than having you both down here because of *this*. Once they catch him, we could all take a trip down to San Diego for the weekend, maybe – or at least for a Saturday, since I've got to study. Or maybe we could take a chartered boat out around Marina Del Rey."

I fiddle with my pen, running the barrel along the edge of my desk. "Well, okay," I say, trying not to sound too disappointed.

"I mean, you can come if you'd like – I'd love to see you, of course, Mom – but I just don't want you to feel like you need to come down here for *this*. I'm just going about my business at school like nothing happened, anyway."

I twiddle my fingers together, thinking. I'm worried about her, and I feel left out up here in San Francisco all alone, but she has a point. It almost seems like overkill; me canceling my appointments for the next several days just to fly down there and stay in a small motel room with Bruce while our daughter studies and sees us for dinner at night. Like she said, the idea of coming down there to celebrate would be much more fun. I like that idea more.

"Alright. I hate to admit it, Annie, but you're right." I grin.

"I know I am."

"But you two had *better* keep me filled in on all the details. I want to be updated as soon as you find out any information. Promise?" I raise an eyebrow, giving them both a stern look.

"We promise," Bruce says, nodding his head.

"Yeah, of course, Mom," Annie agrees.

"Well, you both look great. Have some fun tonight if you've got time. Do some touristy stuff."

"We would, but I've got to go over some reading material tonight for class tomorrow."

I nod, giving her an understanding look. "School comes first. I get that. Well, you both get some rest and I'll do the same. Love you both."

"Love you too," they say together. I smile at them and press the X button to end the call. When their faces disappear from my phone screen I feel a little empty inside as I sit all alone in our house. I miss having her around already, but I know she's a grownup now and it's time for her to be out on her own. The thought makes me smile even though I feel a bit sad about it all.

Well, at least I don't need to go through the frustrating process of calling all of my clients now. That means I've got a free night tonight to sit here at home and do whatever I'd like. And what I'd like to do is make some popcorn and watch some movies. That sounds like a perfect night.

A couple of hours later I'm sitting on the couch with an empty bowl of popcorn on my lap as I sit there staring at the screen with heavy eyelids rising and falling. I'm trying my hardest not to fall asleep, but despite the movie being a good one, I'm having a hard time winning that battle. I yawn, stretch my arms out, and stand up. After putting the bowl in the dishwasher, I head upstairs to bed. When I lie down, I close my eyes and then quickly open them once I hear something.

It sounds like footsteps. Soft, careful footsteps. The footsteps of a person who is tiptoeing and trying to go unnoticed but is too heavy to do so.

Someone is in the house.

Chapter Thirty-Three
Bruce

As much as I wish Judy were down here with me, I'm glad that Annie managed to talk us both out of making this a bigger ordeal than it is. Sure, I know that Tony being here is something that raises legitimate concerns, but what good would it do to have Judy cancel all her upcoming training sessions in order to come down here and join us as we fret over it? In what way would her presence down here in Los Angeles help the situation?

I haven't heard anything from the police tonight. I was hoping I'd get an update, but I think that was wishful optimism. Well, at least Annie didn't have any weird encounters today. I mean, God, imagine if the guy showed up on her campus? That's what worries me. But I know that sitting here in this little hotel room worrying over it isn't going to help the matter.

I sit up from bed and stretch. It's not a bad hotel room, but it's small, and I feel cramped in here. I think I'll go take a walk. That might end up being productive. It's a decent walk from here to Annie's campus, and I'm feeling up for it right now, so I tie my shoes and walk out the door, then head down the steps and out through the courtyard to the front of the hotel. Then I turn and start walking east through Santa Monica towards the spot on Wilshire Boulevard where Annie saw the creep. On the drive back to her dorm tonight, I had her point me to the exact location so that I'd know where to look.

I have to say, it feels a little bit strange doing this. Not strange in a bad way, but strange in a sort of ridiculous way, as if I'm a kid playing dress-up as a private investigator. It feels a bit silly and performative to be snooping around out here on the street corners, but at the same time, there is nothing silly at all about the situation itself, and so I don't think I'm being over the top in doing this. I'm a father who is worried about his daughter – that's all.

And I'm trying to do what I can to help out.

I don't know if what I'm doing is helping at all, though. But at least I'm trying. And now, as I walk around the spot where she was approached by Tony, I feel a heavy sense of worry coming over me out of the blue. It's as if I can sense him all around me, as if I can still *smell* the creep just as he must have smelled when he stood here trying to talk to my daughter. It's just my imagination, of course, but it feels very real, and part of me is now very glad that Annie managed to talk Judy out of coming down here, because I know the darkness I'm feeling would rub off on her. It's infectious, and I don't want Judy to be overly stressed about this like I am.

No one passes me except for some cars. There is no sign of anyone, least of all the man I'm looking for. I wish there were. I wish he were here right now, strolling down the sidewalk, hoping to catch a glimpse of my daughter – but then spotting me instead. I wonder if he would be frightened to see me. I wonder if he would turn and run.

No, he wouldn't do that. Who am I kidding? He'd probably approach me and start trying to chit-chat and feed me that nonsense about how *sorry* and how *changed* he was. Then, like before, I'd threaten him, call the police, he would turn and leave, and the cops wouldn't find him. Just like before. As I imagine it, a gut-wrenching sense of hopelessness suddenly engulfs me.

Los Angeles is a big town. What if they never find him?

Chapter Thirty-Four
Judy

I grab my phone from the nightstand as quickly as I can and dial the police as I try to slip off the bed and sneak into the closet without making a sound. The house is dark now. As always, I turned off all the lights downstairs before making my way upstairs to our bedroom, and after crawling into bed I flipped off the lamp on the nightstand beside me like I always do.

A bit of moonlight creeps in through the cracks between the curtains. Other than that, it is pitch black in the bedroom.

The soft, careful footsteps grow louder as they grow nearer.

"911, what is your emergency?" As the voice of the dispatcher comes on the line, I don't dare reply, because suddenly the sound of footsteps stops as a lumbering shadow appears in the bedroom doorway. I peer out through the thin crack between the closet doors, feeling as if I am too frightened to even breathe.

Why didn't the security alarm go off?

I turned it on just before sitting down to watch my movie.

Was he already in here before that?

A thought so chilling would normally make my skin crawl, but my skin is already crawling as I stand here in the dark corner of the closet peering out through the crack, watching, waiting, and dreading what might happen next.

The massive shape suddenly steps into the bedroom from where it stood waiting in the doorway. I can hear deep, muffled breathing. I am scared to even let out a breath of my own as I stand there with wide eyes and a hand over my mouth. I've turned the volume down on my phone. I'm sure the dispatcher is asking me if I'm okay, but I'm not able to hear them. I didn't want to risk the intruder being able to hear my phone.

Will they have triangulated my location by now? Are police cars on their way? Please, please, *please* let that be the case. Let them get here within the next five minutes and end this real-life horror situation I've suddenly found myself in.

Sweat drips down my neck. My eyes feel like they're going to pop out of my head. I can almost hear my heart beating as it pulsates rapidly in my chest. He stands there in the center of the bedroom, staring down at the bed, and then he reaches for the blankets and pulls them down a bit, only to drop them back down onto the mattress, as if he had been looking for someone hiding beneath them. Then he turns slowly and stares towards the closet.

Time seems to stand still as I watch him staring in my direction. He doesn't move an inch. I can't read his expression. It's far too dark in the room to be able to see his face, and he is facing away from the window where the little slivers of moonlight seep in. I wish I would hear police sirens. I wish I would hear the doors being kicked down, and voices shouting: "*Police!*"

But I don't hear any sirens. All I hear is a cricket as it chirps on one of the trees outside the bedroom window. I hear a car with loud exhaust as it drones by on the next block. I hear the faint sound of a happy couple laughing outside on the sidewalk below as they pass the house without a care in the world, and without any knowledge that a woman is in here hiding in her closet, in dire need of help.

He comes closer to the closet, taking three quick steps before suddenly stopping. He keeps his gaze on the closet doors, scanning them up and down. I can see now that he has a ski mask covering his face. He takes another step. My heart seems to stop. I gulp slowly and wonder if I should close my eyes and accept my fate.

Then I open them and feel a sudden surge of defiance. *No. If he finds me, I won't die without a fight.*

I look up and try to think of anything that might be feasibly used as a weapon. There are coat hangers, a couple of small, fairly heavy boxes filled with jewelry that I could possibly crash over his head, but there is nothing else I can think to use. I lower my gaze and watch as he stands there unmoving, staring ahead towards the door. Does he know I am in here? Can he hear me breathing? Can he smell me? I used a leave-in conditioner tonight – maybe he can smell it.

He turns suddenly and goes out of the bedroom and down the hall. I hear him opening Annie's door. I hear his footsteps walking all around her room. Then the footsteps stop and I put the phone back up to my ear. The dispatcher is still on the line. I can hear his voice as I press the volume button, turning it up. I don't even dare whisper, but I want to hear what the dispatcher is saying.

"...Should be there shortly."

He has to be referring to police, of course. Hearing those words makes me want to melt with relief, but I'm not out of the woods yet. Suddenly, the sound of footsteps starts up again, and so I turn down the volume on my phone and put it in my pocket as I look down and reach for a jewelry box. I pick it up and hold it up above my head as the footsteps come into the bedroom. Then they stop.

For at least two minutes, there is no sound, and from this angle, I can't make out where he is. He is out of my line of sight. I try my hardest, but I can't see him through the crack between the closet doors. He must be standing just out of sight, perhaps by the wall – but why is he doing that?

Does he know I'm in here?

Suddenly, he appears directly in front of the closet door. His muffled, heavy breathing fills my ears as he puts a hand on the knob and begins to twist.

And then stops.

The sound of sirens have filled the air. It is the sweetest sound I've ever heard. They are close. Within a minute they'll be here.

I stare straight ahead through the crack at the intruder who stands less than a foot from me outside the closet door, and I watch as he quickly turns and runs from the room.

Chapter Thirty-Five
Annie

Sometime in the early hours of morning my phone begins to ring. I'm sleeping so deeply that I hardly notice it until Jaylyn groans grumpily from her bed across the room. I grab it wearily from the nightstand beside my bed and pull it to my face, mumbling into the line. "Hm?"

It's Dad. He sounds incredibly upset. Suddenly wide awake, I bolt upright with the phone pressed firmly against my ear and listen to his quavering voice.

"Honey, I've got something to tell you. Mom's alright - she's fine - so don't worry, but there was a break-in at the house tonight. I think it was probably him. It was probably that creep from New York. I just needed to let you know I'm on my way up there now."

"What? Dad, what's going on? I'm so confused."

"I'm sorry for startling you like this in the middle of the night. There was someone in the house last night, Annie. I think it was him. It had to be. It was Tony. Thank God the police got there in time. Mom was hiding in the closet. He came in the bedroom and was looking for her. She could see him through the crack between the closet doors. He had on a ski mask, so she couldn't make out his face, but he was a big guy. He must've been watching us down here, Annie. You and me. He knew that I was still down here around LA and that Mom was alone." Dad's voice quakes with anger, and then he releases a long, trembling breath. "I just needed to let you know that I'm going to drive back up to San Francisco now to be with her."

"I can't believe this," I mutter.

"But like I said, Mom is fine. Just rattled. The police are with her now. He won't get another chance for that to happen. He must've been in the house for a while before she set the security system on the doors and windows."

I don't say anything. I'm too stunned to speak. My mind is reeling with images of him lurking around our dark house while Mom sleeps soundly. This phone call could have gone so much differently. I'm so glad that Mom ended up being okay. I'm glad he didn't get to her.

"Well, I don't think I'll be able to sleep much now. Do you think I should come up to San Francisco, too?"

"Oh, no, honey. Of course not. You stay and focus on your studies. Things will be fine. Mom's fine, too. She's strong, you know that. That little snake isn't going to be able to hurt her now. I talked to Lieutenant Morton, and he said he's going to have a squad car posted out front of our house for the next few days. Who knows if he'll even stay in San Francisco, though – I was shocked at him coming down to LA to begin with." Dad pauses. I can practically hear him grinding his teeth together anxiously. "I don't think he's going to show up back down here, though. Regardless, we'll see what the police say and if they're able to locate him. It only just happened a couple hours ago, so he must still be in San Francisco. They'll find him. His luck is running out." Dad sounds like he's trying to be encouraging, but I'm not sure if I agree with him. Somehow this man has been able to go undetected thus far, and with him being as careful and sneaky as he is, I don't see that changing. I can't imagine him getting caught – not unless the police decide to give us bodyguards, which of course, is a laughable idea that they would never consider.

But after breaking and entering our home, I think things might be on their way to changing. At least the police will take it very seriously now.

I hope.

Chapter Thirty-Six
Bruce

The sun has long since risen by the time I reach San Francisco, but it's hidden beyond a veil of dark clouds. Rain looks like it is approaching, and a heavy fog rolls in from the sea, covering the city in a shroud of mist. There are two police cars parked out front, plus an unmarked car that I know belongs to Bill Morton. I'm thankful that he probably has stayed here all night and kept an eye on things. He's a good man.

I swerve into the garage, hop out of the car, and run up the front steps to the door. I've never been more eager to see my wife than I am now. As I barge in through the front door I see two young officers standing in the foyer. Their eyes widen when they see me, probably wondering who I am, and they start to speak but suddenly Bill turns the corner and calls my name, putting their worries to rest.

"Bruce, you look like you haven't slept a wink."

"Hardly. Where's Judy, Bill?"

"Asleep upstairs. Been up there for several hours snoozing away. The boys and I have been down here just waiting for you to arrive. Everything is under control, but there's no sign of him." He frowns.

"It was him, Bill. It had to be."

A hesitant look slowly fills his face. He holds up both hands and says, "Now, wait a second, Bruce. I think it was him too, but we're going to follow the proper procedures and make sure of that. Right now we don't know for sure. It could have been unrelated. There were a string of robberies several months back a few blocks from here. Whoever it was rummaged through a chest of drawers in the living room and stole some watches and jewelry. That's what Judy told us. We had her check. The drawers were all pulled out and things were strewn across the floor." He pauses, scanning my face. "It could've been a simple robbery, Bruce."

"Or made to look like one. He was here for her. I'm sure of it."

"Could have been. I'm just saying we've got to not get ahead of ourselves here."

"He came into our bedroom. She told me he did. He was looking for her. He knew I was gone and so he came back up here from LA and went after my wife, that's what he did. Who knows what he was going to do to her, Bill? But I can guarantee you it wasn't anything nice he had planned."

"I'm not saying the intruder was up to any good, Bruce. All I'm saying is we don't know for sure it was the man you're after. Give us time to figure that out."

"She said he was big."

"A lot of people are big, Bruce." He pauses, sensing my frustration, then puts a hand on my shoulder. "Buddy, we're on the same page. I think you're probably right. I'm just trying to calm you down. We've got to follow protocol. We'll find this guy regardless, okay? Whether or not it was him who came in here tonight, we'll find him."

I stand there and have to prop myself up against the wall. I feel exhausted and dizzy, and now the annoying back and forth is making my blood pressure rise. I don't know why he seems so reluctant to admit it's obviously him. Clearly, Tony was the one who broke in here. That explains why I haven't heard anything from the LAPD regarding his whereabouts – because there was no one to find. He headed straight up here, didn't he? He came up here to stalk my wife, to break into our house, and do God knows what to her.

But he didn't. Thank God, he didn't get the chance.

"Buddy, you should go upstairs and get some sleep as well. You need it," Bill says. "As for us, we're going to have a car staked out down here for a couple days like I told you over the phone. I'm going to get some shuteye myself, and then I'll come back by later on and check things out. We should have some intel by then if all goes well."

"And if it doesn't?"

Bill stares at me. "We're going to do everything we can to find out who did this. He didn't make it easy. He was wearing gloves and a ski mask. But you can rest assured that you two will be safe here. I'll see to that."

How can he guarantee our safety? And if he's right – if he's right about this possibly being unrelated to Tony, and simply being a robbery, then what about our daughter? What about Annie, all alone down there in Los Angeles?

"Bill, you know I just came here from LA. You know why I was down there, too. I called you and told you, remember?"

"I know." He nods.

"So, what do you expect me to do now? I come up here because a man broke into our house and was looking for my wife, and now you're telling me it's maybe not the guy I think it is."

"Bruce..."

"Which means he's still down in LA."

"You've got to relax, buddy. I'm not saying it wasn't him, but I'm saying we don't have proof that it was. We accessed records of your boy's prints from New York. Those prints couldn't be found anywhere near the house."

"Well, you said he was wearing gloves, so that explains that."

"Exactly. Which means we don't have any evidence that it was him, other than a feeling. I think it was him, too, Bruce. But a feeling certainly isn't a substitute for proof. We've got to have proof he was here."

"Oh, hell, what does it matter anyway? Just find the creep, will you?" I throw my hands up. "Neither you nor the cops down in LA have been able to do anything for us. Not a thing. This guy's been roaming around for two months now, breaking his parole, and what do you do? Nothing."

Bill sighs. "Bruce, there's nothing we *can* do if we can't find the guy. I'm sorry. Like I said, we're on the same page. I think it was him, but there's a chance it wasn't, also. We don't have proof right now, but we're working on it. It could've been whoever pulled those robberies several months back. And if it *wasn't* him, then I think that should come as a relief to you."

"Why would that come as a relief to me, Bill? All that it would mean is that he's still down in LA near my daughter. Now I don't know where to go or what to do. Christ, I'm being spread so thin here by bouncing around the state, and I'm not even doing any good. I haven't accomplished anything."

My heart races as I stand staring at Bill and the two younger officers behind him. I haven't even gone up to see Judy yet. Without saying another word, I turn and hurry up the steps. I feel sick thinking about this. I pause as I reach the second floor landing and brace myself up against the railing. It doesn't seem like Bill is taking this case as seriously as I thought he would. Either that, or the two of us are on completely different pages. He thinks the guy was a mere robber.

But I don't buy that. It had to be him. We've never been robbed before. Never had any sort of break-in. Why now? What are the odds of it happening now, right at the same time that we've been dealing with this creep?

It can't be some random robbery.

My pulse jumps up and down like a rollercoaster as I stand at the top of the staircase dripping with sweat. A disturbing thought comes to me. What if I'm wrong? What if Bill is exactly right? What if this was a random break-in and nothing more?

A million different thoughts zip through my mind. I don't know what to think anymore. I feel almost completely defeated. And now I'm worried about Annie, because if Bill is right, then that means Tony never even came back up to San Francisco.

He might still be close to her.

Chapter Thirty-Seven
Judy

I feel cold fingers running along my cheek. A man wearing a ski mask gazes down at me. His eyes look blank. I see the fabric of the mask crinkling up around the mouth, twisting into the shape of a smile. A broad, sadistic smile. The smile of a man who has nothing left to lose.

My eyes snap open as I start to scream before stopping myself.

It is only Bruce. He gazes at me with a look of worry in his eyes.

"Honey? It's me."

"I was having a nightmare," I say.

"It's okay. You're safe now. I'm home, and the cops are downstairs. Bill was here all night, you know?"

"Yeah," I sigh, closing my eyes and lying back down onto the pillow. My eyes stay fixed on the ceiling. "I stayed awake for a long time talking to them, answering all kinds of questions." My eyes move to Bruce, who is hunched over beside the bed. "I thought I was going to die last night. I thought he was going to kill me."

"Was it him, Judy?"

I shake my head. "I don't know, Bruce. I told them a million times; he was wearing a mask. He was big, that's all I know. He was tall and broad. It was so dark in here."

"Like overweight, or muscular?"

"Muscular, I think. But he was wearing a long sleeve shirt. A black shirt. I don't know." I sit up in bed and stare at him. "How is Annie? I wish you'd stayed with her."

"I came here as soon as you told me, honey. You know I couldn't leave you up here all alone after hearing something like that. Do you think it was him?"

"The man who kidnapped Annie?" I ask softly before looking away, pondering the question. "I don't know. I feel like it was him, but it was dark, Bruce."

I feel immensely frustrated right now. Not with Bruce, who I know is only worried and trying to help, but with the situation we're in. It's as if our lives have suddenly been flipped upside down. And, like Bruce, I'm very worried about Annie.

"You don't think it was him?" He sounds disappointed with my answer as he stares deep into my eyes.

"I don't know, Bruce. I couldn't see his face. I couldn't see anything. All I could see was that he was big."

Bruce lies down beside me and crawls under the sheets. "I'm just so tired," he says. "First he was here. Then he was in LA. Now he's back here – if it even is him. I don't know what to think."

"I don't either." I rise and slide my feet off the edge of the bed, letting them hang there with my back turned to Bruce. I can feel him staring at me from where he lies.

"He's toying with us, Judy. He's toying with us, and he knows it."

I turn and look at him out of the corner of my eye. He's lying there gazing at me. His face is ridden with anxiety. "Do you think Annie is safe on campus?"

"I think at this point, we don't even know where the man is. He could be here; he could be there. But he can't be everywhere, Bruce, and neither can we. So please get some rest. We'll figure out what the game plan is later on, okay? Maybe both of us will head down to Los Angeles and just call it a vacation for the next week, and we'll just see what happens."

I stare at the window but don't really look out of it. My eyes feel glazed over and I am deep in thought, thinking about whether or not it was him. I feel as if it must have been, but I don't want to say for sure. It's not as if there isn't crime in the city, because there is, but I just don't buy into it being a coincidence. Not now. Not with that man lurking about in the shadows.

But I don't want to worry Bruce with that. I know he's worried enough as it is. And in all honesty, if it *was* him, I think it's a good thing. Because that means he's no longer in LA, and Annie will be safe. Unless, of course, he chooses to simply drive back down there. But that's utterly ridiculous. He can't keep driving up and down the state just to *toy* with us, can he? Just to string Bruce along for the ride? I don't see it. To me, that sounds like crazy, erratic behavior.

But then again, behaving crazy and erratically makes perfect sense for a person like him. After all, he doesn't seem to be all there mentally.

Bruce begins snoring softly beside me. Despite how worried he is, I know he needed rest, and I'm glad he managed to fall asleep quickly. I'm sure his anxiety put up a fight, but the fatigue won out in the end, and when I look down at him, I smile a bit. He looks so peaceful with his eyes closed and his lips gently pursed together. I watch him taking slow, shallow breaths as he slumbers, and I think about how badly I want peace to be brought back to our family.

We had it so good for a while. For seven years, things kept getting better and better. It seemed as if things were going perfectly until that man showed up. I don't even like to say his name. I don't even like to think about it. It makes all the little hairs rise on my skin. Even the mere thought of him makes me begin to shudder. So I try to think of other things. Happy things.

I think we'll take a walk later. A long walk through the city with Bruce sounds nice. But first I'll let him sleep. Then maybe we'll pack our bags and get one more good night's rest here in town before heading down to Los Angeles to be near Annie. I'll talk to Bruce about it and see what he thinks. I know it's probably meaningless, but it will make both of us feel better to be near our daughter until this stalker is apprehended.

If he is apprehended.

Chapter Thirty-Eight
Annie

My classes for the day seem to pass by like a waking dream. It's tough, because I know I should be paying attention, but I'm finding it hard to do so. All I can think about is Mom, and how worried I am about what happened. I had called earlier, right after getting off the phone with Dad, but Mom hadn't answered me. I didn't panic, though, because I know she was still with the police or asleep. Hearing that the cops were going to be parked out front made me feel better, too. But I just wanted to hear her voice. Hearing the story secondhand from a very panicked father made it hard to follow.

I don't understand how this could have even happened. If it was Tony, then why would he go back up to San Francisco to do that? What does he want with Mom? Or does he just want to hurt our family in general? Maybe Dad is right – he went back up there after realizing Dad had stayed down here with me. He's been watching us, somehow, without us knowing, hasn't he? God, I hope we're wrong about all of this.

As frightening as it might be, I hope it was an unrelated intruder. Just a robber, nothing more. A man who thought our house looked nice and unsecured and figured he would try his hand at taking valuable things out of it.

Maybe it's as simple as that. I don't want it to be Tony going after Mom.

Or maybe I am being blissfully naïve about it clearly being him.

It's four o'clock now, and I'm finished with classes for the day. Despite all the stress I'm feeling, I can't help but smile when I look up at the blue skies of Southern California. I wouldn't mind going out tonight with Jaylyn just to clear my head. She had sent me a text earlier mentioning it. Something about going to get some coffee or dinner somewhere, maybe in Santa Monica or Venice. Neither of us have class tomorrow, so why not? I deserve a bit of a mental break from school, and from the chaos of what's been going on with my family.

And it's not like I'm going out *alone*. He isn't here in town, I'm sure – if he went all the way back up to San Francisco last night, I'd say he's hiding somewhere around there – but I still would feel a bit leery about going out alone tonight. Being with Jaylyn at least puts my mind at ease. If the creep *were* still in Los Angeles, I don't think he'd have the guts to approach me if I'm with someone.

And the thing is, it makes me irritated to even have to try and justify my leaving campus. It's ridiculous, and I'm not going to let myself live in fear of this creep. That's clearly what he wants. He's taunting us. He's angry about what happened to him and how his life was ruined, and I guess he thinks it's *our* fault. I know that's what Dad thinks he's doing, and I don't disagree.

But I'm not going to stay holed up in my dorm feeling dark and depressed in the meantime. If I do that, then I'm letting this weirdo win. He's not the ruler of me, and I'm not going to let him intimidate me to the point of not going outside, other than to my classes.

A couple of hours later Jaylyn and I are sitting in a café enjoying some tasty treats. We just had dinner at a Mexican restaurant and then found ourselves stumbling into this cute looking café which has delicious coffee, pies, and cakes. I chose apple pie with whipped cream and Jaylyn got carrot cake that she gave me a little piece of.

"I can't decide which one I like better." I laugh. "Yours or mine."

"They're both to die for." She grins from ear to ear and slices through the fluffy icing and spongy cake, then forks another big bite into her mouth as I do the same with my apple pie.

I'm glad we came out tonight. I feel good about it. As soon as we got into Jaylyn's car and started driving here, I started to feel so much better, like a heavy weight had been lifted off my shoulders. Maybe that's a bit over the top, but it really does feel that way. I guess I've been feeling so much pressure as of late – not about school, which I'm loving so far, but about this weirdo bothering my family.

Mom called me during dinner. She didn't want to talk long since she knew I was out with my roommate, but I insisted on keeping her on the line for a while because I'd been so worried about her. I wanted to ask her many questions and make sure that she was okay. She sounded fine, which was kind of surprising. She also told me that Lieutenant Morton had just spoken with her and Dad and told them many little details he had found out about Tony. I know she was shaken up by what happened, but as she said, it could have ended much worse. I hope I have inherited some of her mental strength. She sounded so resilient as we spoke. But maybe she is just putting on a strong front so that I don't worry about her.

    It's funny because I do the same for them. But I know they're both frightened about this, and of course worried about me. I feel bad for Dad, because now he's so worried about *both* of us. He's a good guy, zipping up and down the state trying to protect us - trying to be everywhere at once. I don't want him to feel like he has to do that, though. He's not a superhero. He's a great dad to me, but I don't want him to have a heart attack from stressing himself out over this.

    All things considered, though, I feel like after what Mom went through last night, it can't get any worse. The cops are finally taking it very seriously after that. Or at least that's what she told me. She and Dad seem to think that they'll find the guy soon. It's kind of hard to believe that they will, but in the grand scheme of things, it has hardly been any time at all since he confronted me here in LA, so I know I can't expect them to work miracles. Things take time to play out. I'll have to be patient, and so will Mom and Dad.

After our dessert, Jaylyn and I ride back to campus. I watch the city lights flash by; all the strip malls and houses and offices look like a blur to me as Jaylyn cruises down Santa Monica Boulevard and then takes a left towards Wilshire. I'm feeling blissfully content until I suddenly glance over to see Jaylyn peering incessantly in her rearview mirror. Her worried eyes seem to be spending more time looking at the mirror rather than the road ahead of us.

"What is it?" I glance back and see nothing noteworthy behind us – just several other vehicles, which is to be expected in a car-centric city like LA.

"Nothing," she says dismissively. After a beat, she glances up at the mirror again and says, "That's weird..."

"Huh?" I turn and glance behind us again. There is nothing strange that I notice. Cars are behind us, which of course is normal in any city, especially one with traffic like LA. But for the moment, traffic is moving smoothly. And yet, if Jaylyn keeps her eyes glued to the rearview mirror, that might change any second. I nervously stare ahead to make sure we're not about to run into anything. "What is it?" I ask again.

"That truck has been following us the entire time. Or at least ever since we turned out onto Santa Monica Boulevard after leaving the coffee shop. And no, I wouldn't imagine something like that."

"Seriously?"

"Yeah. But maybe they're just going the same route as us."

I turn in my seat and peer behind us. It is a silver truck with dark tinted windows. I don't think much of it at all. It just looks like a regular truck you'd see anyone driving. Los Angeles has plenty of mid-sized trucks on the road. And like Jaylyn said, maybe they are just taking the same route as us. It's not like we took many turns. We simply took Santa Monica Boulevard the entire way until turning onto the street we're on now.

"It's probably nothing," I say.

But as I turn to focus on the road again, the truck suddenly veers out from behind us and passes us noisily; the diesel engine roaring as it spits out a plume of thick smoke.

"Oh, now that's not very nice," Jaylyn says sarcastically.

"What a jerk. Guess you weren't going fast enough for him."

"Oh well. At least that puts my fears to rest about it being some creeper following me. Thought for a minute it might be my ex. He texted me a few weeks ago bragging about some new truck he got."

"Maybe it was him."

Nothing about the truck makes me feel any sort of way. It was just some jerk on the road. Maybe it was her boyfriend, maybe not. I'll have to get used to aggressive drivers now that I'm living in LA. I didn't drive much in San Francisco, but now that I'm here I know I'll be driving a lot when I'm not spending my time studying and in class.

I forget about the truck almost immediately, until we arrive at campus and pull into the parking structure. As we drive up the levels, I notice the truck parked on the second level.

Suddenly, a shiver runs deep inside of me, starting from my stomach and radiating all the way up my spine through my neck and the top of my head. As we pass the truck, I turn and stare at it, and through the tinted windows I see the outline of a man. I can't make him out, but I can see enough to frighten me.

No. It can't be him.

But the feeling I have is horrific. I don't know why, exactly, but I've convinced myself that it's him – that he's following us. That he is waiting for us to park, and then… Then who knows what he's got up his sleeve?

Sure enough, as we make our way towards the next level, and as I crane my neck to keep staring at the truck before it disappears from view, I see the door open and a man steps out of it. But just before I can get a look at his face, Jaylyn turns the corner and veers up onto the third level.

"Wait, don't park," I say. "We need to get out of here. I've got a bad feeling suddenly."

"Huh?" She looks at me like I'm crazy.

"Turn us around. Get out of here." My voice shakes.

Chapter Thirty-Nine
Annie

"Keep driving," I say. "Turn around and get us out of here."

"What?" Jaylyn laughs.

"I said keep driving. That was him, I think. That was the guy the cops came about."

"*Who* was him?"

"The truck. I just saw it parked. I think he was in it."

The smile on her face vanishes quickly. "Okay. Alright, hold on. Let me turn around somehow. It's tight in here."

There are hardly any empty parking spaces, but once she finds one, she quickly pulls into it and then reverses back out of it. A moment later we are descending down the levels. Neither of us speak, and the tension feels thick enough to cut with a knife. I'm holding my breath as we reach the second level, waiting for him to jump out from behind some column and land with a thud onto the hood of Jaylyn's car like a scene in a horror movie. I imagine him slamming his fists on the windshield, shattering it, and falling in on top of us as we scream for our lives…

But that doesn't happen, of course.

We pass the truck, and no one seems to be in it. He is around here somewhere, but I don't know where. I feel that familiar sensation on my skin – the crawling sensation. It's as if someone is watching me and I can't see them.

"That was spooky," Jaylyn murmurs. "You should call the police if you're sure it was him. Report that freak immediately."

But then it dawns on me that I'm *not* sure it was him. Not by a long shot. After all, I only reacted that way based on a feeling. But the feeling of dread I felt as we passed the car was stronger and more unusual than anything I've ever felt before. It was as if for a moment I had some sort of sixth sense telling me to *get out* immediately.

Jaylyn drives us down the narrow road, and I pull my phone out as we approach a green light. Before I get a chance to dial the first digit, Jaylyn suddenly screams. Immediately following the scream, I feel the collision.

A vehicle coming from our right slams directly into the front corner of Jaylyn's car. Her car spins dizzily and then slams up against the curb, lurching to a violent and sudden stop. It all happens in a matter of seconds, and then it is over. It is silent again. There is no more metal scrunching against metal, there is no more vicious screeching of tires, and there is no more screaming.

It is over, and that's when I finally manage to breathe.

I reach up and rub my stiff neck. It's already begun to ache. But my heart is what I'm worried about – I've never felt it throb with such intensity.

"Are you okay?" Jaylyn asks from the driver's seat.

"Yeah. Are you?"

"Oh, God. My grandpa gave me this car. I didn't even see that car coming. That moron ran the red light!" She shouts.

I look ahead and see a small sedan with a demolished front section.

"He ran the red light," Jaylyn says again. "Now my car's probably totaled." She sighs and then throws her hands in the air and then quickly swings the door open and steps out onto the street.

I feel a mixture of relief and embarrassment. I am by no means happy that we've been in a car accident, but I thought we'd just been hit intentionally by *Tony*. I thought he had plowed right into us, and for a second after it happened I imagined him getting out of his truck and hurrying over to our vehicle, jerking my door open and dragging me out of the car kicking and screaming.

But it wasn't that. It wasn't him. It was just some random driver who was probably staring at their phone instead of the road in front of them. It wasn't Tony. It was just a random accident, and thankfully both Jaylyn and I are okay.

But then a wave of sudden embarrassment starts creeping over me, and after several seconds I'm completely consumed by it. What if I'm to blame for this accident? I freaked out in the garage and told her to get out of there. We wouldn't have been in this position if I hadn't told her to get out of the garage. We'd have parked and...

And he'd have attacked me, most likely. Just like he did seven years ago in another parking structure three thousand miles away. I think that's what caused me to suddenly panic a few minutes ago – when we pulled into the parking garage and I saw that truck, all those memories came tumbling back into my head and I freaked out for a moment, thinking it was him, thinking he was going to try to take me again.

But what if I was wrong? What if that *wasn't* him?

What if his taunting of my family is starting to get to me? What if I'm starting to lose it? What if the person driving that silver truck was just some random student here at UCLA? Maybe I just had a panic attack.

I only know one thing for sure – this situation is starting to wear on me mentally.

The cops come, statements are made, insurance cards are exchanged. Jaylyn is still grumpy, and understandably so, but the driver of the car that ran into us is at full fault for the accident, and so she won't have to pay a penny in the end, I hope. Still, seeing her car so messed up is a real downer.

Especially considering I'm starting to feel guilty over it.

I sit here on the curb and stare out at the campus. What a night it's turned into. It was such a great day, and then bad luck seemed to come right after we laid eyes on that stupid silver truck. I shake my head as I think about it, then I get up and walk over to Jaylyn. She had mentioned to the officer that I thought I'd seen Tony in the garage, but the officer hadn't seemed particularly interested in handling more than the crash report. I decide to tell him again, just to try and get him to take us seriously. He shakes his head and chuckles. I really don't like his personality.

"Okay, okay. I hear you, just relax. You say you saw a man named Tony, and yet... you aren't *sure* you saw him, so... What am I supposed to do with that?" He lets out a tired sounding sigh.

He's trying to make me feel foolish, and I'd be lying if I said he wasn't halfway succeeding.

"I don't know. I just thought it was him." Hearing myself say these words suddenly makes me feel so self-conscious. I notice Jaylyn is also giving me a weird look, or is it my imagination? It's like they both aren't taking what I'm saying seriously. Maybe they think I'm crazy.

He frowns. "Okay, well, if this *was* the guy that has been stalking your family, at least now you know what truck to look out for. Shame you didn't get the plates, though. We could maybe get somewhere with this if you had. Silver trucks of that make are a dime a dozen in LA county."

An hour later I'm taking a hot shower and trying to calm down a little. My mind has felt ridiculously overwhelmed ever since having that little panic attack in the parking garage. I regret telling Jaylyn to get out of there – I wish I'd been braver and told her to park. But I can't help how I reacted. I've never panicked like that before.

Was it even him?

I feel so stupid now as I think about it. After drying off and dressing myself I figure I'll go back to the room and talk it over with Jaylyn. I hope she's not mad at me, but I got the feeling that she was. She didn't say anything, but it's just the way she looked at me that makes me think she doesn't like me now. Maybe I'm just feeling paranoid about things, though.

Jaylyn is gone when I get back to the room. She seems to have lots of friends, so that doesn't surprise me. I'm guessing she went out to blow off some steam about the whole accident. I don't blame her. She must feel pretty down in the dumps now about everything. So do I.

I sit on the bed for a second and feel restless. I should try to get some sleep, but I feel wide awake. However, looking down at a bright phone screen isn't going to help that one bit, so I figure I'll plug my phone into the charger, lie down, and close my eyes. Even if I don't feel like sleeping, I'll just lie here and try to turn off my brain for a while. Maybe I'll be able to sleep eventually if I do that long enough.

As I slip myself beneath the sheets and get nestled in, I reach over for the charger and hook it up to my phone, but I notice that it doesn't seem to connect. I try it again. No luck. I reach down and unplug it from the wall, then thrust it back in and give it another shot. Again, it doesn't charge. My phone is at seven percent battery right now, which means it'll likely be dead by the time I wake up, which also means I'll sleep through my alarm. Great. The last thing I feel like doing now is wandering out into the parking lot to get my spare charger from the car, but I know I need it, so I don't really have a choice.

    I crawl reluctantly out of bed, pull on my shoes, head out the door, and stroll lazily down the hallway towards the elevator. The air feels crisp and chilly as I walk out through the front doors towards the parking lot. There are several people out and about, which makes me feel a bit safer. I normally would feel perfectly fine while walking alone through this lot at night, but there is still a creeping sense of paranoia in the back of my mind, and I can't help but feel as if I'm possibly being watched.

    And yet, I know that in all likelihood, the probability of me being watched right now is slim. In fact, that silver truck I saw earlier could have belonged to someone else. I don't like admitting that, but ever since the car accident, the possibility has been eating at me, and I feel like I'm responsible for Jaylyn's car being totaled. Sure, the person who is truly responsible is the driver who ran the red light, but we wouldn't have been at that intersection to begin with if I hadn't flipped out in the parking garage.

I can't seem to stop dwelling over it and replaying it in my mind. Was it him, or was it someone else? The more time that passes, the more I start to think that it was someone else, and that I simply had a panic attack related to some sort of undiagnosed post-traumatic stress disorder from seven years ago that suddenly revealed itself when Jaylyn and I went into the garage and I saw the truck.

So maybe I did end up causing the accident in a way. No wonder the cop was looking at me like I was crazy. And Jaylyn's expression wasn't much nicer, either. Ugh, she must hate me right about now. Maybe they're both right.

Maybe I've simply gone a little crazy. Maybe all this stress has caused me to snap.

But as I walk through the parking lot towards my car, my worries about having lost my mind vanish in an instant as soon as I see Tony stepping out from behind a vehicle some five feet in front of me.

"Hi," he says softly, staring at me with wired, unblinking eyes. "Can we talk?"

Chapter Forty
Bruce

I've felt so close to Judy today. Something about that horrific event last night seems to have brought us even closer together, reminding us again of the fragility of life and how it can potentially be taken away in an instant.

Not that anything like that happened, of course, but it could have. It *could* have – and the realization of that makes me feel completely devastated as I stand here leaning up against the kitchen counter with a wine glass in my hand. I could have lost my wife last night.

In fact, it seems like I came very close to that happening.

He was in here. Right here in this house. Right inside our bedroom within a foot of her, with a thin closet door being the only thing separating the two of them. I shudder to think about what might have happened if the police had shown up a minute later. Would Judy still be here now, lying on the couch, head cocked to the side, gazing at me with a playful smile?

I love her smile so much. I love everything about her. Sometimes I don't think much of myself as a husband, but I hope she always feels that I am good to her, because I would die for her, as I would for our daughter. Not that I am planning on that happening. I would much rather be able to stick around for a good while longer and grow old with Judy as we watch

Annie grow into whatever career path she chooses. No matter what, I know I'll be proud of her.

I take another sip of wine and set my glass down on the counter as I smile at Judy. She spoke with Annie tonight, which ended up putting my mind at ease. I was a bit worried initially to hear Annie say she was out at dinner with her roommate, but I know I can't be a domineering parent. If I act like one, then I know she will resent me. She is eighteen now and on her own. And the police calmed me down earlier when I spoke to them. Bill Morton came back over and had a friendly chat with Annie and me.

They monitored surveillance camera footage around several surrounding blocks, but the footage didn't tell them much. After a couple of blocks they weren't able to track him any further. All they could see was that he walked north and then they lost him after that point. But Bill says he spoke with an old, retired friend down in LA who used to be a detective, and the man said he'd speak with some colleagues who were still on the force. He might be able to escalate things and get some more cars patrolling the area around UCLA. Not that I think Tony is going to go *back* to Los Angeles after coming back up here, but at this point, nothing would surprise me. Having a bit of extra security around my daughter would make me feel so much better.

He also told us some details on Tony himself. Apparently, he inherited a high five figure sum of money from his grandmother while incarcerated. This explains why he was able to travel to California from

New York and have a mode of transportation. They're still working on identifying what kind of car he may be driving. There is nothing registered to his name in New York, and it appears that he may have purchased something in cash off the books.

From what Bill says, though, he has a valid license which in fact was one of the first things he make sure to take care of upon release. It seems as if he went straight to the department of motor vehicles and renewed it, and then upon receiving it in the mail he wasted no time in booking a ticket to California and at some point bought a vehicle right after arriving. There are no credit cards to his name, which makes tracking him hard. He must have withdrawn a large sum of cash from his inheritance upon release.

And, just like anyone would have predicted, he is indeed violating his parole by coming here. I have to say, hearing Bill confirm that fact put a big smile on my face. Simply because it means that once he is apprehended by the law here in California, he will be extradited back to New York, where he will undoubtedly be sentenced once again to prison for violating parole. Call me unsympathetic, but I won't lie, it makes me feel happy to know that this creep will be locked up again. And I am sure that if they can tie him to this break-in, then he will get extra time tacked onto his sentence. A lot of extra time. Once he is behind bars, which I hope will be soon, I'll make sure to open up one of our nicest bottles of wine and pour a glass for Judy and myself.

Because once he is behind bars, I think I will finally be able to put this worry behind me and forget about him once and for all. It'll be a grand celebration.

I just hope there are no more surprises between now and then.

Chapter Forty-One
Annie

I take a step back before finding the strength to speak. He holds up his hands and makes a frightened face.

"Get back or I'll scream," I say, glancing quickly from side to side. The people I saw walking through the parking lot moments ago are now nowhere to be seen.

It's just the two of us.

He backs up; his eyes widening. He waves his hands and says shakily, "I would never hurt you. I'm not the person I was before. I just wanted to talk. Please. We don't have to go anywhere. We can just talk right here, right now. I won't come any closer, okay? I promise." He pauses, staring at me, his wide, fear-stricken eyes searching me up and down. He looks just as frightened as I imagine I myself must look.

He suddenly continues, blurting out: "I saw the accident tonight. I was there when it happened. You knew it was me following you, didn't you? I'm so sorry. I know that comes off as weird, but I don't mean for it to. I know this isn't right – it's not right to follow someone, I mean – but I can't live with myself until I know you've heard me out and accepted my apology. I did something so horrible back then. I know I was just a kid, but I still should have known better. It's been tormenting me since I found God."

"What do you want from me?" I stammer, taking another step back. "You just want me to forgive you? Okay, you're forgiven. I forgive you. Is that all? Can you go now?"

He looks down towards the ground and shakes his head as he makes a sad face. "You don't mean it. You still sound so angry, so scared. I don't know why you won't give me a chance. I don't know why you can't seem to accept the fact that I've changed. You know people can change, right? Especially if they did bad things as a kid and learned from their mistakes. My brother was a monster. I loved him, but he was a monster."

"I said you're forgiven," I snap back at him, nodding my head as I stare wide-eyed at him. I wave my hand. "You can go now. Okay? You're forgiven."

"Why are you so scared of me now? I'm telling you the truth. There is no one else around right now. If I wanted to hurt you, I'd reach out and do it. It would only take me a few seconds to reach you from where I stand. But you see I'm not moving. I'm not *going* to hurt you, okay? I don't have any bad intentions. I swear."

"You were in San Francisco last night, weren't you? You broke into my family's house."

His mouth twitches a little as he stares at me, blank-faced. He shakes his head as his brow furrows with confusion. "Annie, I don't know what you are talking about. San Francisco? I left San Francisco months ago."

"You lied about having a job here, so I can't trust anything you say. You said you were hired by a company that helps reform prisoners, but that's not true, because you're violating your parole in New York. The police told my family that. They've spoken with the police in New York. You're in big trouble just by being here. You should go. Please. I don't want any trouble. Please leave my family alone now, okay? You're forgiven."

He stares at me for a moment with a severe look of desperation on his face. Finally, he nods his head and sighs. "Yeah, I lied about that. What else was I supposed to say? That I'd followed you and your father down here from San Francisco? You'd think I was crazy if I told you that. I just wanted to speak to you in private, because *you* are the one who deserves the biggest apology. I want you to know that I am so upset over what happened seven years ago. It should never have happened. I just wanted to come down here to tell you in person, one on one, without your parents influencing your decision whether or not to forgive me. I know they mean well. They think they are protecting you from me. But they don't see the full picture. I've changed. I really have."

"I understand that," I say, hoping that he believes me even as I lie through my teeth. "I told you I forgive you. You're forgiven. Really, I mean it. I accept your apology, I really do, okay? I promise I'm not just saying that to make you feel better."

He stares searchingly into my eyes with pursed lips as he slowly nods his head. Then a smile fills his face, not unlike the smile of a child on Christmas morning. "You mean that?" He asks, sounding overcome with joy.

I feel a little crazy for thinking this, but maybe this man isn't dangerous after all. At least not anymore. The thought seems completely absurd, but in all honesty, he looks like a lost child right now, staring at me with watery eyes and trembling cheeks. Despite his intimidating physique, I couldn't imagine this man hurting a fly.

But even if he has been genuinely asking for forgiveness all this time from my family and me, that doesn't change the fact that I feel a deep sense of discomfort when he is near me. The feeling is so strong that it makes me wish I could vanish into thin air just to get away from him. I feel frozen here with the soles of my shoes stuck against the pavement. If I simply turned and began to walk away, would he come after me?

And what if it's all an act? What if he's not sorry at all? What if he's just having fun bothering me?

He clasps his hands together in front of his face and closes his eyes before letting out a deep, gasping breath, as if he has just come up for air after a long dive. "You really mean it, don't you?" His eyes open. He lowers his hands. The smile remains fixed on his face and spreads from ear to ear. "I knew that if I came here, it would do some good. I knew it would bring me some inner peace to hear you say those words and *mean* them. Thank God for you and for your forgiveness. I don't know how I can explain to you how much it means to me, Annie."

"It's okay," I say, nodding slowly. "You don't have to explain. I understand." I hope desperately that he will leave me alone now.

He keeps smiling at me but eventually seems to pick up on the fact that I'm uncomfortable. He chuckles and waves his hand towards me.

"Well, I guess I'd better let you get on with your life, then. I don't have anything else to say, really." He tilts his head back a bit, staring up above me, as if he is trying to think about whether or not he has anything else on his mind that he wanted to tell me. I feel the hair on my arms start to stand up when he looks back down at me.

Something is very wrong with this man.

The grin is still on his face, but it looks completely empty, like it's all a show with nothing genuine behind it. "I guess all I can say is that I appreciate your patience more than you'll ever know. I want you to know that prison did me good. I changed in so many ways in there and learned so many things. Please tell your parents this, as well. Tell them I'm very sorry. I don't think it would be smart for me to attempt to tell them myself. Your father would not be nearly as patient as you have been with me." He sighs, then looks down at his shoes before glancing up at me again. "Thank you, Annie. I'll get out of your hair now. You won't have to worry about seeing me again. I suppose once I turn myself in, I'll be looking at a bit more time for violating my parole."

He shrugs. "But it was worth it to make things right with you. Goodbye."

He turns and walks through the parking lot. I stand there frozen as I watch him drift through the sea of parked cars before arriving at his silver truck several aisles away. I watch as he gets into it, starts the engine, and pulls away.

Is that it? I wonder.

I stand there for a while longer, letting it all soak in. Then I walk to my car and grab my spare charger. I put it in my pocket and make my way back through the parking lot.

I don't know what to make of that – any of it. But I know that without question, it was one of the most uncomfortable and awkward social interactions of my life. And yet, despite that, it felt strangely genuine to listen to him standing there politely rambling to me – until the last smile he gave me. There was something very off about that. I didn't like listening to him ramble, but I prefer him being an awkward weirdo to my initial fears of him being a dangerous maniac.

Above all else, though, it feels like the end of things, once and for all.

But then I hear the roar of an engine from behind. As I turn and squint, blinding headlights bore down on me. The silver truck comes barreling in my direction as I turn and begin to run.

But it's futile. Even a gold medalist sprinter wouldn't stand a chance.

The truck speeds past me and then comes to a twisting, screeching halt in front of me. The door swings open and Tony jumps out and grabs me before I even get a chance to react. He hoists me up into the air and starts carrying me to the truck. I kick and scream as he sets me on the seat and leans in close to hiss in my ear: "Keep screaming and I'll drive up to San Francisco and put a bullet in your father's head while you watch with your eyelids taped open. Then I'll put a bullet in *your* head while your mother watches. After that, I'll let her join the two of you. A happy, loving family, laid to rest. How's that sound? You still want to scream?"

The words slither off the tip of his tongue as he sneers, and after that, I keep quiet, because I know he isn't bluffing. Or if he is, it isn't a risk I'm willing to take. He pushes me over into the passenger seat and flashes a shiny gun tucked into his waistband. Then he smiles before crawling up into the driver's side. He twists the key into the ignition and the truck's engine roars to life as he slams his foot onto the gas pedal.

"I don't think I need to repeat myself, do I? I think you're well aware of the consequences of trying to escape or causing a scene, are you not?"

"Yes," I say softly.

I don't want my parents to die, and I know that if I don't follow his orders, he won't hesitate to kill them violently.

"That's good. That's very good. Your parents raised such a nice, well-behaved young woman." He glares at me as we reach a red light. "Now, we're going to take a little *trip* together. Just the two of us for the next six hours. If you are good, then *I'll* be good. If you are bad, well..." He flashes the pistol again and grins at me. "I swear I'll do it slowly. I'll make the three of you beg for death."

The next few minutes feel like a waking nightmare. This cannot be happening. Eventually we end up on the freeway heading north. I know where he's taking me, but I don't know what is going to happen when we get there. I don't bother asking him. He's a lying psychotic, and whatever he tells me likely wouldn't be the truth.

Fear begins to squeeze me like a vice. It makes it hard to breathe or think straight. I try to calm down. I try to rationalize what's happening.

But there is nothing to rationalize in his behavior. He's going to take me to my family home and kill us all, isn't he? And there is nothing that I'm going to be able to do about it.

I look out the window at all the passing cars and think about how my plight is unknown to all of them. I'm just another faceless passenger in another of the endless vehicles riding along the freeway. No one knows I'm being held against my will. No one knows I'm sitting next to a homicidal maniac.

I'm all on my own now. No one is going to help me out of this mess. And when we arrive at Mom and Dad's house in the middle of the night, neither one of them are going to be prepared for this. I hadn't even bothered telling them about the crash with Jaylyn and seeing Tony's truck. I didn't want to worry them.

I close my eyes and try to think.

There has to be a way out of this.

Chapter Forty-Two
Judy

After a nice dinner at home with Bruce, we sit in the living room and put on a movie, but both of us seem too tired to pay much attention to it, and when he starts drifting off beside me, I reach for the remote and turn off the television. Then I nudge Bruce and take him by the hand. "Come on, honey. Let's get some sleep."

He smiles dreamily and sits up from the couch, yawns, and stretches his arms out as he walks behind me towards the staircase. I still feel shaken, as anyone would, after what happened last night, but I also feel stronger than I did before. I don't think anything else will happen. Not after that. The cops are taking it very seriously now, whereas before they seemed to be casually dismissive of the severity of the threat. I guess it took a household break-in to wake them up.

If it even *was* him. The thought bothers me a little. What if it was just a random intruder? I don't know which I'd prefer. As I lie down in bed beside Bruce I ponder the question. Which would be more ideal? The break-in being a random intruder, or Tony? No matter what, it's a horrifying thing to experience, but I suppose I would rather it have been Tony, if only for the fact that it means he is no longer in Los Angeles and chose instead to drive up here and fixate himself on me rather than Annie. I'd much rather be his target than her. It would break me if something were to happen to our daughter.

Bruce is already asleep beside me. Today we both took off from work, of course – that went without saying – we both needed some mental and physical rest after what happened. And in the morning we'll pack our bags and get a late start on our trip down to Los Angeles. We still haven't told Annie that we made up our minds about coming. I didn't want her to be put off by the idea or think that we were going to behave like helicopter parents, watching her every move. Bruce and I will also do some things alone together while we're down in Southern California; things like hiking while Annie is in class.

But mostly we're going down there because it will give us some peace of mind, of course. There's no denying that. It's obvious to both of us that we'd feel more secure about things if we were around Annie, even if it doesn't do any actual good. It's not like it is going to hurt.

I try to close my eyes and fall asleep, but my mind feels restless. I keep thinking of Annie, Bruce, and of last night. I keep thinking of how everything has gotten so crazy out of the blue. And it's a shame that it had to happen in the first place. Seven years have gone by and our wounds from that time in New York City had mostly healed. Then he shows up and cuts those wounds wide open again by bringing back all those treacherous memories.

But at least Annie is safe, and so are we. There is still a police car parked out front. I hope that the officers sitting inside of it are awake. The thought almost makes me chuckle as I lie there, but I manage to hold it in, because I don't want to disturb Bruce. He's sleeping like a baby next to me. I quietly get out of bed and wander on tiptoes over to the window. Drawing the curtains apart, I stare out at the street below us. I can see the police car down on the street, parked right in front of our house.

I close the blinds and walk back over to the bed, lying down in it and curling up beside Bruce. As I wrap an arm around him and pull myself close, I feel his warmth against mine. I smile softly as I lie there beside him, feeling content.

We had a big scare, but nothing like that is going to happen again. Tomorrow, the three of us will be together as a family. We'll wait it out together until the police sort this thing out.

It doesn't take long for me to fall asleep.

Chapter Forty-Three
Annie

We roll into San Francisco well before dawn. The sky is a milky shade of purple as we turn onto the street I grew up on. A police car sits perched out front of our house.

"Get *down*," Tony bellows. "You try anything and I'll kill you right where you sit." He pulls the gun from his waistband and aims it up at me, scowling.

I hunch down in the seat, hiding my head from view. I feel my heart racing as I stare down at the floorboards and panic, wondering what is going to happen next. Despite it being a six hour drive up here, I was unable to think of any possible way out of this situation.

Are Mom, Dad and I as good as dead?

I can sense Tony's tension as we drive slowly past the house with the police car parked in front of it. He looks as if he is holding his breath. As we turn the corner, he drives around the block and slowly comes to a stop, double-parking on the next street over.

"I'm going to get out of the truck. You will get out after me and keep quiet. I'm sure I don't need to tell you what will happen if you don't follow my command."

I nod my head. He stares at me with an icy gaze for a moment, then he gets out of the driver's side and walks around to the passenger side. I open the door and get out, standing beside him. He turns from side to side, surveying our surroundings. The streets are desolate. It's too early for morning joggers, and we are the only ones around.

"Call your parents," he says suddenly. He sounds enthusiastic.

I hesitate.

"Call them. Tell them what's happened and tell them to come outside and meet us on this street. Tell them to dress up like they're going on a jog – that way they won't alert the two officers sitting out front of their house. But before you tell them this, be sure to make them aware of the fact that if they call the police or alert the two officers sitting out front, I will know. And that foolish mistake will result in a bullet in their daughter's head. Okay? If you'd like *me* to speak with them instead, I'd be glad to. But I think they'd appreciate hearing the fear in your voice. I think that would help sell the seriousness of the situation." A sneer spreads out across his thin face. This is fun for him.

In his eyes, it's all a big game.

"My battery is almost dead," I say. "If it's not already."

"Oh, stop making excuses. Pull your phone out of your pocket and *call* them."

He thinks I'm lying, but I'm not. I pull my phone out and look at it. The battery is two percent. Hopefully that'll be enough for a phone call. I almost wish it wouldn't be. I don't want Dad and Mom to get roped into this situation. I'd rather be the only one to suffer today. I don't want to die, but I don't see how bringing Mom and Dad into this is going to make my chances of living any more likely. It'll just mean we'll *all* get killed.

"*DO – IT,*" he hisses furiously.

Hesitantly, I raise the phone to my ear after pressing Dad's name in my contact list. I chose to call him instead of Mom because he always keeps his phone on the nightstand beside the bed. Mom sometimes keeps her phone charging downstairs because she likes to be away from it at night. The phone rings several times and then Dad comes on the line.

"Annie?" He sounds half asleep and very confused. He clears his throat. "Honey, is everything okay? What's wrong?"

I tell him.

For a moment there is no sound on the line. Then, I hear him swallowing. "Oh, my God. Okay, honey. We'll be right out. I love you. Don't – don't worry. This is going to be okay. I'll fix this." His voice sounds stiff. He is trying to sound calm and rational to make me feel better, but I know he must be terrified of what I've just told him.

"Wait, *wait*. Give me the phone," Tony snarls, snatching it from my hand. He holds it up to his face and clears his throat. "I don't think it's necessary to tell you who this is. You know I have someone very precious to you and your wife. There is no use in beating around the bush. I'm going to play it straight with you, okay, Bruce? If you even think about calling the police before you come outside, your daughter will pay the ultimate price for that little mistake – her life. You know I'm not bluffing. I've got a gun pointed at her stomach right now and I have nothing to lose." He looks at me and hands the phone over. "*Tell* your father I've got a gun pointed at your stomach," he says sternly, glaring at me.

"He has a gun pointed at my stomach." I feel sick as I say it.

"Honey, tell him we are not going to call the police. We'll do what he asks. Please put him on the line again," Dad says.

I hand Tony the phone. He sighs, holding it up to his face as he says, "You'd better get dressed, the both of you, and be out here in five minutes. I'm growing more impatient by the second."

I can hear the sound of Dad's muffled voice on the line even though the speaker isn't turned on. He sounds frantic. I'm sure he's begging for my life now; pleading with Tony to not hurt me.

"Just do what I ask and no funny stuff. Do what I ask, and your daughter will live to see another day. And maybe you will too, Bruce, if I'm feeling generous." He ends the call and grins as he hands me back my phone. "I trust you don't have plans to use that phone to call for help. You noticed I didn't bother taking it away from you on the way up here, right? That's because I know you're not stupid enough to try and do something like that. Right?"

I nod my head as he glares at me.

I can imagine what Dad must look like right now. He must be wide awake and dripping with sweat after that phone call. He is probably reaching over the bed now to rouse Mom and tell her the news. I feel a sense of terror rising up in me, even more intense than the terror I felt on the long drive here. I have been awake since yesterday morning, and yet I feel wired due to the fear surging through me.

I feel the cold barrel of the gun suddenly press up against my shoulder. "You're looking awfully fidgety. Thinking of trying to run? If you try anything, I'll shoot you in the spine. Do you know what would happen then? You'd be unable to move. You'd be lying there bleeding out while you watched me finish off your parents. You don't want that, do you? It sounds like a nasty way to go out, doesn't it? Nod your head if you agree."

I nod. "I'm not going to run."

"Good," he says. "I knew you were smart."

I remember once, after my grandfather passed away, being curious about how I would end up dying one day, but I never imagined that day coming so soon. I pictured myself curled up in bed, taking my last breath in the middle of the night while sound asleep, dying peacefully without even knowing it was coming.

It's looking like I was wrong about that, and as a bit of orange begins bleeding into the purple sky, I close my eyes and hope, more than anything, that my parents and I won't succumb to whatever this psychopath has planned for us. But no matter how hopeful I try to feel, it doesn't seem to help. The reality of the situation sunk in during the long drive here, and now that we have arrived at our destination, all I can seem to think is that my family and I won't be waking up tomorrow.

If I were alone right now, I'd take off on foot and try my best to run away. I know it probably wouldn't work, but I'd try. But I can't do that. Not with my parents involved. I know he'd shoot me dead and then they'd come out of the house a moment later to meet us around the block like he told them to, and then he'd kill them. I can't let that happen.

Think. Just calm down and think. There's got to be a way out of this.

But no matter how much thinking I do, I can't seem to devise any sort of plan. I wish this were like a movie, where the main character stays calm and collected and thinks of a way out of the slippery situation they've found themself in, but I can't think of any way to get out of this. Not unless the three of us rush him at the same time, maybe. But what if he shoots one of us before we get ahold of him?

I can't lose Mom or Dad.

How fragile life is. One minute Mom, Dad and I are here on earth living, breathing, and laughing, and then the next minute a deranged lunatic can choose to put an end to all our combined years of existence.

I'm not ready to say goodbye to life yet. Not today.

Chapter Forty-Four
Bruce

"You folks okay?" The cop seated in the passenger seat rolls down the window and leans his smiling face out.

"Going on a little morning jog."

"Early risers. Whew. I couldn't do anything except for sit here and sip coffee at this hour, let alone run." He checks his wristwatch and chuckles. The cop behind the steering wheel is leaned up against the window and seems to be sleeping.

"Yeah. We always like to run in the mornings," I lie.

"Okay. Have a good one. We'll be out here 'til the morning replacement comes."

"Thank you," I say.

I glance over at Judy. She looks frightened, but she hides it well from the police by forcing a smile and a little wave. She and I are both dressed from head to toe in fitness gear – spandex shirts, running shoes, nylon pants. I even threw on a headband to make it look more convincing. I didn't want the police to get any sort of idea that something was wrong.

We walk together down the sidewalk. My heart pounds as we turn the corner and see the two of them – Tony and Annie. She looks distraught. All the color has gone from her face. What has this maniac done to her? I break into a jog and then start running at full speed towards her, but Tony pulls out a gun and waves it at me.

"Whoa, there, Bruce," he says, letting out a quiet whistle. "Hold your horses, pal. Don't act so impatient. I don't like when people are impatient." He aims the gun away from me and with a flick of the wrist points it up towards Annie's face, pressing the tip of the barrel against her temple. "When people are impatient, I tend to get trigger happy. You don't want me to get trigger happy, do you?"

"No, please. Please don't hurt our daughter."

"Cut the corny pleading. You do what I say, she doesn't get hurt. Now, you see that truck double-parked to my right? You and your wife are going to get into the back seat and sit together holding hands – all four hands interlocked. I'll be watching you in the rearview mirror as I take us all on a little drive. I'll be steering with one hand, because my other hand will be a little busy aiming this gun at your daughter's head. If I see you and Mrs. Hurt let go of each other's hands at any point, the gun goes off. Understand?"

"Don't hurt her," Judy pleads.

"We understand," I say.

It is a cold morning, but I am already caked in a heavy layer of sweat as if I've gone on a run through the city on a summer day. As we get into the back seat of Tony's truck, I feel nearly delirious. This was not how I expected any of this to play out. This was never in a million years a scenario I thought we would find ourselves in.

Waking up to the sound of my daughter's voice describing the situation was the biggest wakeup call of my life, and my mind is still reeling from it.

Part of me is silently praying that I am still in bed having some sort of demented nightmare, but the other part of me knows that is not the case. This is real. It's happening, and if I don't find some way of stopping it, my wife and daughter are going to die.

There is no way he's going to let either of them live.

Not unless I find a way to stop him.

But as for now, I don't even know where he is taking us. I feel feverish with fear as he drives us through the sloping hills of the city and then past the outskirts towards the coast. After a while I can smell the sea and even hear the tide as it rolls up onto the boulders and the sand. Dawn is fast approaching, and as cars pass us in the opposite direction on their way into the city, I wish they knew what we were facing. I wish somebody would help.

I wish I had a sign to hold up against the rear window of the truck: *CALL POLICE. KIDNAPPED.*

But I *don't* have a sign saying that, and if I did, I don't think I'd be able to risk displaying it. Not while Tony has a gun pointed at my daughter who is sitting helplessly in the passenger seat. And even if I did, it's unlikely that anyone would notice it in time. The idea of someone suddenly appearing to save the day is highly unlikely, and if there is any way out of this, then it is going to be up to us to find it, because no one else is coming to help us.

We're on our own.

The truck passes the edge of the city limits. We roll on along the twisting turns of the Pacific Coast

Highway for what feels like thirty minutes in silence. Every once in a while Tony will glare at me in the rearview mirror, and his eyes will dart down as he checks to make sure that Judy and I still have our hands locked together. Just like he told me, he keeps one hand on the wheel with the other hand aiming the gun at Annie.

    I have never felt such anger in my heart, such ill will towards another human. I imagine what I would do to him if I were able to unarm him. I might lose any shred of humanity I still have left while acting out in a fit of rage. I might not be able to control myself.

    I might kill him with my bare hands.

    But that is just wishful thinking. I'm well aware of the fact that Tony has the upper hand. He has all the leverage, and all I have are dark revenge fantasies keeping me going. I wonder where he is taking us. If I could just find a way to get him distracted for a moment, where he stopped aiming the gun directly at Annie… Maybe I could snatch it from him.

    Suddenly, he veers off onto the coastal side of the highway. I stare out at the scenery ahead of us. It is a tranquil, desolate spot that in happier times would be a pleasant setting for a family picnic. A ring of trees surrounds a little green clearing, and just beyond it is the cliffside. Below the cliff the tide roars as waves crash in against the rockface.

Tony cuts the engine and puts the keys into his pocket. His eyes lock with mine in the rearview mirror. The gun is still pointed at Annie.

"I'm going to get out of the vehicle first along with Annie. Then you two get out on the same side and stand there. Any sudden movements and I will fire. Understood?"

"Yes. Please – we're not going to try anything. We just want our daughter," I say.

"Shut up," he says, gently wrapping his finger around the trigger. His eyes widen. They swivel slowly over to Annie. "You're going to crawl out of the driver's side after I get out," he says to her.

She nods. He opens the door and cautiously backs out of it, waving the gun at Annie as she slowly crawls out after him. Judy and I follow suit, stepping out from the back door together. I wrap a hand around hers and gently squeeze it as if that might offer some sort of encouragement, as if I'm telling her that we're in this together and that we're going to get out of it together, too.

But I don't know if I even believe that myself.

Chapter Forty-Five
Judy

Tony stands there with the gun raised at Annie. The barrel is level with her midsection. He sneers at us gloatingly. "Ahead of me. *Go.* Lead the way. Walk until I tell you to stop."

Bruce and I walk out past them and together we slowly walk into the small patch of grass with the ring of trees surrounding it. We are about ten feet from the edge of the cliff.

"Stop," Tony's voice calls out from behind. "Turn around."

He presses the barrel against Annie's back. "Walk. Keep walking and everything will be okay."

Annie walks. Tony scowls in our direction as he slowly passes us, walking behind Annie, his gun up against her spine. "Your parents are playing nice this time. Not like back in New York. Not like when they called the police and messed things up for all of us. Not like when they got my brother and I imprisoned. Not like when my brother got knifed in the yard. This time Bruce and Judy are doing exactly what I ask of them. *Stop.*"

Annie stops.

They are standing about five feet from the edge. He waves the gun at Bruce and says, "Nice spot for a special family moment, isn't it? Nice spot to have some reflection on the things you've done. It's really a beautiful spot, Bruce. Not such a bad place to call it quits, if you know what I mean. I'd miss these fun little interactions the four of us have had recently if this were to be the end of them, but this really isn't such a bad spot to end things."

A sickening nausea comes over me. What is he talking about? Is he going to shoot us all and then himself? I can't stand here and just allow that to happen without putting up some sort of fight. Or maybe I can reason with him. I know he is insane, but couldn't it be possible for me to redirect his anger towards us rather than Annie? He is angry at us for what happened seven years ago. He is furious that he was caught and imprisoned, but Annie was only a child. She had nothing to do with that.

"What – what do you mean?" I stammer. "Please, just… *Please*, listen to us. Don't hurt our daughter. She had nothing to do with any of this." Despite my desperation, it is difficult for me to get the words out. I'm choking on my tears. Bruce squeezes my hand.

"I like this spot a lot. I bet my brother would've liked it too. He never got to see much of the outdoors. Always a city guy. Born and raised in New York and never really got much of a chance to leave, you know what I mean?" He waves the gun around a bit but never lets the barrel stray far from Annie. His jerky movements are making me nervous, and I think that's his intention. "He was always busy working, hustling, trying to provide. That's what an older brother has to do when we've got two lowlife drug addicted losers as parents. That's what has to be done in that kind of household. Grandma was good, but she was just one person, and one person can't fix everybody's problems." He pauses and clenches the gun tightly with his hand.

I am not going to let my daughter die like this.
I have to do something. *I have to.*

He chuckles then and shakes his head, smiling past us as if reminiscing about some long lost, pleasant memory. "You know, my brother taught me a whole lot about hard work and making money. He also taught me that sometimes there are people who seem to have all the money in the world. People who don't deserve it. People like you."

His tongue slides across his upper lip as he sneers at Bruce and me. "You could've just forked over the million and got your daughter back. You screwed things up. You told the police when we warned you not to. *You* got me locked up and turned me into a felon and you got my brother killed behind bars. It's all because of you, and you know something? I've been waiting seven years to get out and tell you how much I hate you for ruining my life."

I don't dare utter a word. I don't think he would respond well to hearing either of us argue with what he is telling us. But I try to think of what to do, and sadly, the only thing that comes to mind is suddenly charging him. But how? He has the gun raised in the air and pointed directly at Annie's head. I know that if I try to rush towards him, he will pull the trigger before I take my second step.

And if I did miraculously get to him before he got the chance to do so, then what? Would I tackle him to the ground? I can't do that on my own without likely getting shot, not without some help, and I'm unable to speak right now to Bruce and communicate my plans with him.

I'm hopeless. We're completely at his mercy now, aren't we?

And there's not a thing we can do about it but hope for the best.

"We can work this out," Bruce says softly. "I can sign over everything I own to you. Just give us our daughter. Please. She had nothing to do with what we did to you."

"Just hand her over, huh?" Tony smirks.

"Please. She was a child. A *child*. She didn't call the police on you. She didn't do anything. If you want to blame someone, blame me. Not my daughter, and not my wife. They weren't involved." Bruce pauses. I can see his mind working as I stare at him out of the corner of my eye. "*I* was the one who contacted the police," he lies. "I was the one who went to the police after you took Annie, and I coordinated with them during the entire thing. We planned it all. Planned on sabotaging the handoff of the suitcase with a million dollars in it. I helped the cops set it all up. So come on, Tony. Stop being a fool. It wasn't her – it wasn't our *eleven year old* kid, for Christ's sake. And it wasn't my wife. It was me. It was always me, Tony, and you know it."

I don't know where Bruce is going with this, but based on the way Tony's eye is twitching, he seems to be getting some sort of reaction out of him.

"Let go of her, please. Take me. I'm the only one who *really* deserves to die. I'm the one who is responsible for your brother's death – don't you think? Put yourself in his shoes. Pretend he was still alive. Would he want to waste time being upset at the girl, or at the father? The father who caused all this suffering for your family… Seven long years for you and a life ended for your brother." Bruce pauses and shakes his head. "This is silly, Tony. Come on. Put yourself in your brother's shoes."

There is a long moment of silence where the only sound is the loud roar of the ocean below us and a seagull calling from somewhere up above. Tony has not looked at me for at least a minute. Before Bruce's speech and during it, his eyes had been darting back and forth between the two of us, but now they are fixed firmly on Bruce, and Bruce alone.

Annie stands beside Tony; the gun aimed at her, and she closes her eyes. The fear on her face is almost palpable, and yet she also looks determined, focused. Or maybe she simply looks like she has given up and is waiting for the bullet. I know she is horrified, and so am I. I wish for nothing more than to be able to hold her in my arms and carry her to safety.

I wish more than anything that I could somehow miraculously rescue her, but I can't.

Or can I?

He isn't looking at me now. His eyes are still on Bruce, who stands by my side. Maybe that would give me the second I need to get a running start, and by the time his eyes moved towards me and realized what I was doing, it would be too late for him to react. Maybe I could tackle him to the ground and give Annie the time she needed to run from harm's way.

Maybe.

The harsh, fragile reality of the situation sinks in once more as Tony speaks, interrupting me from my delusional, heroic thoughts. "I think I know what you're doing, Bruce. You're trying to make me mad at you instead of your daughter, aren't you? That's it, is it? You trying to make me mad at you? Well guess what? I'm already mad at you, you idiot. And killing you won't bring me the joy I feel compared to killing the ones you love the most and watching your reaction to that. That moment – that sweet little moment – will bring me more joy than you could ever imagine. Stop moving." Bruce has taken a step towards them. "Take another step and I swear to you, she won't even feel it coming. She'll be dead before she hits the ground – or the rocks below us. You want that, Bruce? You want them to have to send a search and rescue team down there to try and find her?"

"What do you want?" Bruce begins to cry. "What do you want?" He collapses to his knees and, sobbing, clutches his face as he screams. "I'm begging you."

"*That's* it. That's what I wanted. I wanted to see those tears. That's what I wanted. Bravo, Bruce, bravo." He chuckles. "Now look at me Bruce. *Look* at me."

Bruce looks up at Tony. Tony's eyes flicker to meet mine for a second before moving back down to meet Bruce who is shaking on his hands and knees. "I want you to remember the pain you caused me every morning when you wake up. I want you to remember this face every night before you go to sleep. I want you to remember the lives that were ended as a result of your actions. It's time, Bruce. Time to say goodbye."

It is now or never. He is going to kill my daughter regardless, and I won't be able to live with myself if I simply stand here shivering as I let her die. I have to do something. I have to move.

I have to *try* to stop him, because if I don't, Annie will be dead, and we all know it. There is no use in standing here trying to appease him with my obedience. He is going to kill her anyway.

It's time to act.

As I take off, it reminds me of my days in high school on the track team running short distance sprints. The one hundred yard and two hundred yard dash – that was my specialty.

And now, as time seems to move in slow motion while I take the first frantic step towards them, the feeling is not unlike it was back in those days, except now there is a real, tangible urgency behind the running. I'm not after a gold medal. I'm not after the approval and praise of my track coach.

I'm after my daughter. And I'm going to run like an Olympic sprinter to save her from this vile psychopath.

I break out into a delirious sprint – head lowered, eyes fixed firmly on my target, arms bent at the elbows as they rise up and down at my side with each step – and watch as he suddenly jerks the gun away from Annie and points it instead at the side of his own head. A maniacal grin spreads quickly across his lips.

Then I hear the sound of waves crashing and the gun going off simultaneously. His body topples backwards and plummets off the edge of the cliff.

"Mom!" Annie embraces me.

I squeeze her so tight, feeling like I can't let go.

Chapter Forty-Six
Annie

Mom and Dad won't stop crying as they hold onto me. I won't lie and pretend that I'm not crying as well. Any moody feelings I ever had as a teenager disappear immediately as I hug them. I thought I was never going to see them again. I thought that it was the end of all things I've come to know in this world. I thought my life was over.

"Are you okay?" Dad asks. I've never heard him sound so vulnerable. His voice cracks, rising and falling as he struggles to get the words out. "Oh, God, Annie... I'm sorry this happened."

"Yeah. I'm okay, Dad. We're all okay now. It's over, isn't it? He's dead," I say wearily.

It all happened so quickly. The muzzle was pressed up against me and then suddenly I felt him pulling it away from me and aiming it at himself. It happened so quickly that for a moment I could hardly comprehend it, and now that it's over, it's *still* hard to fathom.

Why did he do it? Why did he torment us so much? What kind of satisfaction did he gain from it? Was it simply the desire for revenge? That's all? He took his life over that, over the petty desire for revenge on my family?

We stand in the clearing, the three of us forming a ring not unlike the ring of trees surrounding us, and we remain like that for a while as the ocean breeze wafts against us and the sun rises high in the sky. A sense of melancholy comes over me as I relive the last seven or eight hours spent with this maniac.

I could lie down and fall asleep right here, right in this clearing, even with the cold wind making my skin shiver. But I know sleep will come later, after answering many questions from the police and a long, hot shower following those questions. I can't wait to turn on the steaming water and sit under it, closing my eyes as I try to meditate, as I tell myself that there is nothing left to worry about.

Life can get back on track now. All that's left for me to do is forget about that nightmare of a human being.

The police come and go as I sit there on the grass and nod my head *yes*, shake my head *no*, tell them this and that, and go through the motions like I am sleepwalking until they've asked all their questions and close up their notepads. Then Lieutenant Morton drives us home, cruising slowly along the highway as he looks over at us with sympathy and concern.

"Well, it's over, folks. You were put through hell and back, but it's over, and I hope by knowing that it's over you find some kind of comfort."

I stare out at the ocean as we drive along the coast and then the city as we make our way through it. Before long we've ended up in front of our house, and I get out sleepily and wait for Mom and Dad as they sit in the car a minute longer talking to the lieutenant. I close my eyes and lean up against a tree, feeling like I've been awake for days. It's only been just over a day, but that's long enough, and all the adrenaline and fear has made it feel longer than that.

But now I can sleep soundly; I'm sure of it. Now that the nightmare is over and he is dead, I can close my eyes after lying down in my childhood bedroom and fall asleep and have pleasant dreams in knowing that everything is going to be okay.

In knowing that we're safe now. That it's finished. That he's not going to pop up on the sidewalk one day when we turn the corner and start ranting about how sorry he is and how much he wants our forgiveness.

"Come on, honey," I hear Mom saying as she puts a hand on my shoulder and guides me up the steps towards the door. Dad is behind her. Lieutenant Morton waves goodbye and drives off slowly down the road. Dad opens the door and we go inside, then I take a hot shower and let the water beat down on me as I sit in the center of the tub holding myself, rocking back and forth.

After that I sleep until evening.

Chapter Forty-Seven
Bruce

There is a surreal feeling to it finally being over, especially considering I thought it was over seven years ago. I thought he'd never come back into our lives. For seven years I thought he would remain a memory – a *bad* memory – and nothing more. I remember the feeling I had a couple months ago after laying eyes on him for the first time in seven years. Seeing him outside of my office and hardly recognizing him at first before it suddenly dawned on me. It wasn't a pleasant feeling, but I didn't think that two months later he would still be after my family.

And for what? Just to taunt us? Just to wear me down mentally? To make me break down in tears? Was that his final goal – to see me sobbing and pleading for my daughter's safety? Was that why he put the gun to his head and pulled the trigger, because he'd seen enough? Because he'd accomplished all he came here for?

God, what a grim life he led.

I didn't think tormenting my family would be the first thing on his agenda after getting out of prison. But it was. And now, after another horrific situation he brought upon my family, he is gone again.

But this time he's gone forever rather than locked away in a prison cell for seven years.

I can still see the grin on his face; the grin he was giving me as he put the gun to his head. It was still on his face even after he had pulled the trigger. Even as he was tumbling backwards off the edge of the cliff overlooking the Pacific.

I shudder to imagine that grin still on his face as he hit the water and sank slowly into its cold, dark depths. I don't want to imagine that.

The police have long since gone. For a while they came around asking more questions and taking more statements from Judy and me, making sure they were thorough with everything. I told them not to bother Annie, not now, at least. She was still sleeping. It was exhausting answering the same questions over and over, reliving the same awful memories for the officers as they jotted down notes and nodded their heads.

But now it is quiet in the house, and Annie sits on the recliner staring at her phone while Judy and I sit on the couch staring at the television but not really watching it. The mood is a bit somber, which I guess is to be expected. I'm expecting it to take a while longer before we get over this and feel like laughing again. Right now, despite me being overjoyed to be safe and sound with my family, I still feel rattled by what happened, and all I can seem to do is think about it, remembering all the horrible details of this morning.

"How about some takeout? I haven't seen you ladies take a single bite today, and I know you must be getting awfully hungry now."

"I haven't eaten since dinner with Jaylyn last night. But I didn't even think of food until a few minutes ago. Were you reading my mind, Dad?" Annie gives me a little smile.

It's amazing to me that despite everything, we can still smile right now. Although I know we *should* be smiling after managing to make it out of that mess. Still, it just feels odd, like I'm unable to get my lips to move up into the position of a smile. They feel stiff and pursed now, like they get when I'm very tense about something. And now, of course, I'm incredibly tense, even though it's all over. I guess it's just leftover tension from all the events that unfolded today. But soon I know I'll loosen up, and my muscles will relax a little, and I'll be able to truly smile again from ear to ear and feel like my old self. It might take a little time, but I'm sure I'll get there.

I keep thinking of the moment it ended – the moment Judy began charging towards him as he pulled the gun away from Annie and aimed it at himself instead. The moment I was shaking on my hands and knees, begging him to let her live.

That was the moment all the madness and chaos ended in a flash, and it keeps coming back to me. I shake it off and try to think of other things, happy things, things like Judy and Annie, and my goals for work this year. I hope that I can move on from these dark memories soon. I've got my family, and they're safe and secure. There is nothing else for me to worry about and there is no reason for me to dwell on things.

"I could go for takeout. Chinese, Thai, Mexican, or a couple large pizzas," Judy says, planting a hand on my knee and squeezing it. I turn to see her smiling at me. Seeing her also manage to smile makes me feel as if my strength is returning bit by bit.

They are okay, so that means I am okay. Just breathe. It's over. It's done. He shot himself in the head.

And there isn't any coming back from something as extreme and violent as that.

"Heck, I could go for all four of those. How about I bring home some of each?" I joke. "Couple large pizzas, a few boxes of Pad Thai, a big box of egg rolls, maybe a few bean burritos or enchiladas. What do you gals say?" I raise an eyebrow, and for the first time today, I feel myself genuinely smiling. It doesn't feel like I'm forcing my muscles into the position. It feels real.

And it feels so *good.*

"Whatever you all feel like, I'm good with. I'm so hungry suddenly, and when I'm hungry, I'm not picky." Annie chuckles.

I pat Judy on the leg and stand up. "Sounds good to me. Want to take a stroll with me to pick up some food, then, Judy? I'll need help carrying some of the bags." I pause, giving her a crazed, goofy look. "I was teasing about getting Thai, Chinese, Mexican, and pizza together, but I do think it sounds fun getting at least a couple different things… How about we swing by the Thai restaurant and then go grab a couple pizzas?"

"Do Thai food and pizza even go together?" Annie squints from the recliner, looking at me like I'm crazy. She might be right.

"We're about to find out." I wink.

"Maybe they do," Annie says. "I mean, they're both delicious, so... Why not?"

"Okay, Bruce," Judy says, laughing as she rises from the couch. "Let's go pick up some takeout." She gives Annie a funny look, like she agrees with her that Dad is a little nuts, but that she is used to it.

"You want to join us, Annie?" I ask.

"I'll stick around here and wait, if that's okay." She smiles softly and leans back in the recliner, then takes the remote from the table and flips through several channels until she settles on a dark looking horror movie. She puts both hands behind her head and yawns. "I feel like being lazy. I don't feel like moving much."

"That's okay. You earned it. We'll be back in a bit. We'll swing by the grocery store real quick too and pick up some milk. Need anything?"

"No thanks, Dad."

Judy and I put our shoes on and head out the door. It's a beautiful night in San Francisco. The streets are fairly quiet, the sky is a deep shade of purple, and the neighborhood looks as peaceful as ever while we stroll along the sidewalk hand in hand.

I'm so thankful for Judy and Annie, and for the fact that they're safe now. They're okay. That's truly all that matters to me.

We made it out of that horrible situation, and nothing like that will ever happen again.

Chapter Forty-Eight
Judy

Bruce and I swing by the grocery and grab a half gallon of milk. We walk together through the aisles, occasionally squeezing each other's hands as we silently make our way to the register and pay. It feels strange being here after what we went through just hours ago. I can't believe we're just living our lives again, going through the daily routine as if nothing happened. Not that I am complaining – I definitely don't want to sit in our home and brood about it together. It just feels hard to believe, I guess, that it is over, and that we are walking together to get takeout like it's any normal day of the week.

The feeling is such a wild juxtaposition compared to how we all felt during the early hours of this morning. We're going to go home and enjoy some takeout, and maybe we'll watch a movie together while we eat. Such lovely, peaceful plans for the night.

I think about how it all could have ended up so differently had he not turned the gun on himself instead of my daughter. I don't *want* to think about it, but it is impossible not to as we walk down the busy street towards the restaurant. I think about how if things had gone differently, we wouldn't be here right now, excited for takeout. Who knows what we'd be doing now or if any of us would even be alive.

There is no shame in crying, although I don't want to break down and cry right now. Annie is safe.

Bruce is safe. I am safe. The man who came after our family and tormented us is gone. He removed himself from this world, for whatever reason – maybe he felt he had no reason to live anymore, maybe because he knew he had no future other than prison – but the point is that he is gone and he is no longer going to be any sort of threat to our family. I don't wish violence on anyone, and I wish that he could have been captured by the police and put away, but he *held a gun to my daughter's head*, and because of that, I find it hard to have any sympathy for him. Watching her facial expressions as they stood there at the edge of the cliff was the most pain I've ever felt.

    I think it would be naïve for me to suggest that the three of us are going to move on very quickly from this event. In all actuality, I suspect it will take some time and therapy for us to move on. Family therapy, individual therapy, whatever helps, I want to try it. I don't want Annie having constant nightmares over this. I can imagine myself having those nightmares. But strangely, if she doesn't, it won't surprise me. She seems so incredibly devoted to her studies and motivated by visions of her future career, and I don't think she is going to let this haunt her for very long.

    She's certainly stronger than Bruce and me, that's for sure. I know that the two of us are going to need to talk to someone after this. I can see it in Bruce's eyes. He's trying to be strong, just like I'm trying, but I can still see the pain behind them, and the fear, and regret. I know he wishes none of this ever happened. He always blames himself for problems, but I hope he knows that none of this was a result of his doing. I just know that if something had happened to Annie, he would never have been able to move past it, and he'd have felt guilt for years, as if he had been partially responsible by not protecting her.

"Honey?" Bruce squeezes my hand and for a moment I feel like the world is a little blurry around me until my eyes settle and focus on him. He is smiling very softly but looks worried. "You kind of zoned out for a second."

"Sorry," I say.

"Don't be sorry." He rubs my hand and leans in to kiss me. "It's okay. I'm feeling weird too. You thinking about it?"

"Yeah," I sigh. "Thinking about how badly it could have ended up."

"But it *didn't*," he says. "It's over, honey. It ended up the best way it possibly could have. It's going to hurt for a long time – the memories, I mean – but we're all going to get through it."

I smile and close my eyes. It feels good to have a supportive partner. He and I are going to get through this. And so is Annie. Above anything else, what matters the most is that our daughter is safe, and the fact that she is safe makes me feel so much relief.

"Yeah. I know we will," I say.

"C'mon. Let's go get some food." He smiles.

Across the street is the Thai restaurant. After we pick that up, we will go a couple more blocks down the street and pick up our pizzas. When we left the grocery, Bruce called and ordered the pizza ahead of time so we wouldn't have to wait for it once we got there. I'm glad he did that, because I'm getting borderline ravenous at this point, and I know Annie's stomach must be rumbling as she sits in the living room waiting for us.

    The light turns green and the crosswalk sign gives us the go-ahead. Holding hands, Bruce and I start crossing the street, and I tell myself silently that I won't let myself think about those bad memories anymore tonight. I tell myself that tonight is going to be a fun night spent with the family.

Chapter Forty-Nine
Bruce

With both of my hands carrying bags of tasty goodies to be brought home, Judy and I stand at the crosswalk in front of the Thai restaurant as we wait for the light to change. I'm feeling better and better with each passing minute, and I'm looking forward to getting home and having some tasty food. The question will finally be answered – does Thai food pair well with pizza? Although I already suspect the answer from *me* at least will be an enthusiastic yes. I'm not picky when it comes to mixing and matching different cuisines. If something tastes good, I'll happily pair it with something very different if that something also tastes good.

My phone starts ringing as we walk across the street. I slide the bag up my arm and carry it with my elbow as I reach into my pocket and pull my phone out. It is Lieutenant Bill Morton.

"Hi, Bill. Everything okay?"

"Where are you?"

"We just picked up some takeout. Got some Chinese, some pizza-"

"Search and rescue haven't found a body yet, but they found a gun. It wasn't a real gun, Bruce. It was an airsoft gun."

"What?" My heart plummets.

"It's like a BB gun, Bruce. It fires plastic pellets, not real rounds. Still, I wouldn't try firing one at point blank range at my head. He had to have aimed the barrel past the back of his head if he even pulled the trigger at all. The gun was soaked but everything was intact. It was missing one of its plastic rounds, so he likely did fire it – aiming it just behind the back of his skull and firing off into the air." He pauses. "Bruce?"

I've stopped on the sidewalk. Judy turns and stares at me. She begins to look worried. I feel dizzy and frozen with fear.

"Bruce?" He says again.

"What are you telling me, Bill?"

"I'm telling you that it looks like this guy pretended to commit suicide in front of you and then took a step backwards off the cliff and dropped into the sea below."

"No, he's dead," I stammer. "I watched him pull the trigger and I watched him fall."

"The fall wasn't that high, Bruce. Just over twenty feet and with water deep enough not to hit the ocean floor. He knew what he was doing, jumping from that spot. Must've planned it all out."

"Bill, this is ridiculous." My heart lurches as I stare straight at Judy. She looks mortified.

"We've known each other a long time, Bruce, and I'm telling you; this guy isn't dead. The freak has had a hell of a good time taunting you and your family and he doesn't want to give that up. I'm telling you, he faked his death, Bruce. He planned it all. Planned the spot, probably went down to the water and tested the depths. Now where are you? You said you all just got takeout? Which means you're not home, correct?"

"Yeah. We just picked up the takeout," I say breathlessly. My mind is reeling.

"Okay, that's good. *Don't* go back to your house. I'm heading there now myself because I've got a hunch that your house is the place this creep is most likely to show up at."

"But Annie's there," I say. My voice sounds like a hoarse, sickly whisper.

"What?"

"We left Annie there. She's waiting for us."

I don't hear whatever else Bill says. I drop my arm to the side and let the takeout bags fall to the ground. Then I start to run.

Chapter Fifty
Annie

I'm staring at the television screen without a thought in the world for the first time all day. Until now, even when I slept upstairs earlier, I'd been feeling overwhelmed with thoughts and nightmares about everything that happened. But now, as I sit on the couch waiting for Mom and Dad to get back, I finally feel like I've managed to zone out and block out the negative emotions.

I feel surprisingly good, especially compared to how I felt earlier. I tried all day to ignore the dark feelings I was having and think of light things, but it didn't work. I guess that's to be expected, though. After all, it only just happened. It will probably take a good, long while to truly move on from this in any significant way. And now, as I sit here, I begin to think about it again. I try to focus on the pizza that Dad is probably carrying home right now with a smile on his face, and the fact that I've just started college in Los Angeles and will hopefully have a bright future, but it doesn't seem to help. I just keep seeing that creep's face, and I keep remembering that awful, quiet drive up from Los Angeles to San Francisco, and the sense of dread I felt the entire way.

But again, I guess these thoughts are normal to have. The memories are still so fresh. Not even a day has passed. I don't think even the most peaceful, relaxed person in the world would be able to forget about it so soon. Not right after it happened, at least.

Well, even though I'm thinking about him, it's not like the memories can reach out and hurt me. He's gone. Dead.

And that means I'll never have to worry about him again.

Suddenly, I hear the sound of breaking glass, and a second later, the alarm starts blaring. It is the first time that I have ever heard Mom and Dad's home security system in action, and for a moment, the shock of it causes me to feel frozen with confusion.

That's when I hear what sounds like footsteps crunching over glass. It is coming from the side of the house.

Dad's office.

I know I can't stay frozen any longer. Not if I want to live. Because despite feeling as if I am unable to accept what is happening, I know that there is an intruder in the house.

And whoever it is, I am certain that they don't have good intentions.

I jolt upright and turn, hurrying for the front door. But as I rush towards it, I pass the door of Dad's office and see that the doorknob is twisting. As I slide to a stop on my socks I watch as the door opens. There, right in the center of the doorway, stands Tony himself. For a second I feel frozen again. Not just with fear, but more so with complete bewilderment.

I'm dreaming. This is a nightmare. He's dead.

He shot himself. He shot himself and he fell into the sea.

The smile on his face must be a reaction to the look of horror on mine. Seemingly unbothered by the alarm blaring, he steps into the foyer and starts walking towards me holding a knife. The front door is about ten feet from where I stand. I can't make it in time. He'll be on me in a second.

So I take the stairs which are directly to my right, speeding up them like a kid running from an imaginary monster in the middle of the night.

But this monster isn't imaginary.

My screams echo shrilly through the house as I reach the second floor and fly through the hallway until my socks cause me to slip on the hardwood floor and land with a thud on my back.

Pulling myself up, I turn and look at the landing above the staircase and see his foot appearing past the edge of the wall. It is followed by the rest of his body. He stands there and then turns, clenching the knife tightly in his hand as he stares at me with the same sneer stretched hideously across his thin face. I take a couple of steps backwards and he starts to follow.

I reach out for the doorknob to the guest bedroom and twist it open and then slip inside and slam the door shut, locking it. It is only a simple little lock. He'll be able to bust down the door without much effort, I think. The thought makes my heart race as I grab the edge of the mattress and bed frame and start sliding them towards the door to block it. The knob begins to turn. Then it starts twisting back and forth rapidly. I hear banging on the door and then it stops. I stand there waiting in silence, knowing that he isn't going to give up so easily and walk away. I fully expect to hear a violent crash against the door at any moment now, and I try to prepare myself for that. But when it happens, despite knowing it is coming, it still makes me jump and scream.

I turn, rush over to the window, and slide it up. Then I look down from the second floor at the narrow little alleyway that runs between our house and the neighbor's. The drop is fairly high, but I think I might be able to make it without breaking an ankle.

I think.

I hear him screaming in the hallway as he slams his body against the door. Even with the alarm blasting, his screams are still deafening, and he sounds more psychotic than I ever could have imagined. As he pounds the door and screams unintelligibly, I know I cannot remain in this room. I have to take the chance by hanging from the window and dropping.

I look down again. There is nothing to cushion my fall, but that is a risk I'm going to have to take.

I crawl out from the window as I hear the door beginning to splinter - or maybe I'm hearing the sound of the hinges giving out. Either way, he is going to be inside the guest bedroom very soon, and that means I will be dead in a short time if I don't manage to escape. I grab onto the edge of the window and then drop slowly with my feet kicking up against the brick wall of the house.

Then I hang there, feeling my heart sputtering as I try to take a breath and brace myself for the fall. *Bend the knees and try to tumble. Try to roll. Don't land stiff. You'll break your legs if you do that, and then what'll happen? He'll drop down to where you lie, broken and unable to move, and he'll kill you.*

I take another breath, this one short and frantic, and then I let myself go just as I hear the door crash open.

I land on my feet and promptly roll, and despite that I immediately feel a sharp twinge of pain in my right ankle. Fighting through the pain, I pull myself to my feet and grimace. My ankle isn't broken, but it is sprained, and yet I know I can't allow myself to stop because it hurts. I have to keep going. I look up furtively behind me and see his head poking out the window, a rabid look on his ghoulish face. A moment later his leg is sticking out of the window.

Then I hear screams from inside the house. It's Mom and Dad. They are calling my name.

Chapter Fifty-One
Judy

Bruce runs frantically into the living room and spins on his heels, staring at me with a panicked expression before turning into the kitchen and screaming again for Annie.

"*Annie?*" I shout, turning in a slow circle as I dizzily stare around at the foyer. I run from the office to the living room, to the dining room – and then I hear the sound of footsteps above. "*Annie?*"

Bruce hears them too. In fact, he is already rushing up the steps, red-faced, sweaty, panting. I start up the steps behind him and watch as he stops on the landing of the second floor. A moment later he is tackled to the ground.

Bruce and Tony wrestle violently on the ground, screaming like wild animals and rolling over each other as I hurry up the remainder of the steps until I make it to the landing. I start hitting Tony on the back with clenched fists. He manages to get himself on top of Bruce and straddles him with his legs. His huge left hand is wrapped around Bruce's throat.

Bruce's face begins to turn purple as Tony squeezes.

Tony raises his right hand in the air. In it he holds a knife.

Bruce is clenching his wrist, trying frantically to keep Tony from driving the knife into his chest from above.

"*No!*" I howl.

I grab him by the arm and pull it backwards with all my might. He lets out a deep, guttural moan as I drive my knee as hard as I can into his back. He drops the knife and the pointed tip lodges itself into the hardwood floor a mere inch or less from Bruce's torso. Bruce manages to roll out from under him and stands up, clasping at his throat as he gasps for breath. The purple begins fading from his cheeks as he stares at me wide-eyed and in total shock. Tony shakes me off him and starts for the knife, but I stomp on his hand with the hard leather sole of my boot. He lets out a crying hiss, rises to his feet, and reaches down for me.

Bruce jumps onto him from behind, wrapping his hands around his face and clawing at his eyes. Both men scream. Tony starts running backwards down the hall towards the wall, crashing into it with Bruce sandwiched between him and the wall, causing him to fall to the ground. Dazed, Bruce starts to rise but Tony swings a fist into his jaw and makes him fall back down to the ground. Dizzily, Bruce reaches out for Tony's ankles in a fleeting, last-ditch effort to stop him before collapsing fully onto the floor.

Tony starts strutting towards me, his face scratched and bleeding from Bruce's fingernails, his eyes bloodshot and squinting. I reach hastily for the knife, pulling the tip of the blade from the floor. Then I wave the blade in his direction.

"Leave them alone," Annie's voice rings out from below. I feel my head jerk to the side. She stands there with a knife in her hand at the foot of the stairs. She must have just grabbed it from the kitchen.

Tony smiles and then turns to look at me again.

"Don't come any closer," I say, waving the knife.

He stops and reaches a hand out. "Give me that knife," he says.

"This is the last time you ever try to hurt my family," I say.

"Aw, that makes me so scared," he says mockingly, shivering a little. The smile fades from his face. "Give me the knife," he says again, "or I'll take it from you and kill you even more slowly than I had planned. And first I'll make you watch as I kill your husband." He turns his head and looks down at the first floor. "*And* your daughter…"

"You don't scare me anymore," I lie, hoping I look like I know what I'm doing as I brandish the blade in his direction. "Get down on your knees and put your hands on your head. The police will be here soon."

He grins again and even lets out a little chuckle. Bruce slowly stands up from behind, wobbly on his feet. His lips are bleeding and one eye is swollen. He walks uneasily as if he has a concussion.

"Stay there, honey," I say. "It's okay. The police are almost here, I'm sure."

"Yeah, stay there, Bruce," Tony says, keeping his back to him. His eyes stay fixed on me. "Listen to your wife. You don't want me to hurt you again, do you? Not much of a protector, are you? You can't even protect your own family."

"I'll kill you," Bruce murmurs as he stumbles down the hall, bracing himself against the wall. "I'll never let you hurt my family."

Tony turns and laughs as Bruce nears him. He reaches out and grabs onto Bruce by the shoulder and slings him back down to the ground.

Annie starts walking up the staircase quickly.

"Annie, stay there," I shout. She stops in the middle of the staircase.

"I broke you." Tony smiles down at Bruce. "You're finished. You're pathetic. But I won't lie, your daughter is pretty resourceful, buddy. She might have even managed to get away from me if she hadn't been stupid enough to come back here and try to save Mommy and Daddy. I figure I'll let you lie there on the ground choking on your own blood while you watch me kill her and your wife. Sounds good? How does that sound for an ending to the Hurt family? Sound like a plan, buddy boy? Okay, let's do it-"

I take two steps towards him with the blade raised in the air and bring it down like a hammer, but at the very same moment he spins out of the way as if anticipating my move. But he doesn't move fast enough to avoid the blade entirely.

It slices down the front of his chest, and he lets out a howl of pain as he grabs my wrist and twists it just the right amount. I scream as the blade drops from my hand. Then, quickly, he reaches down for it, snatching it from the ground and rising quickly.

"Stop!" A voice bellows out from the foot of the stairs. "Drop the knife." Lieutenant Morton stands hovering there with his gun raised and eyes narrowed. "Annie, get out of the way."

Annie stares back and forth between Morton and us, and then slowly moves back down the steps and stands beside him. Tony is facing me. His lips are pursed tightly shut, but behind his eyes, there seems to be a faint sense of amusement. Then, surely enough, his lips twist into a big, satisfied grin. As if it is all a game, he lets out a hearty laugh as his tongue dances slowly across his lips.

I know what he is going to do. He is going to raise the knife and kill me right here and now, isn't he? Then, by the time Morton shoots him, it will be too late. I'll be dead. Bruce will be okay, and Annie will be okay too, which is good, but I'll be gone at that point. Dead. Victim of a homicidal psychopath.

And I'm not ready to die. Not yet. Not by this maniac's hand. There is still so much more time I want to spend with my family.

We are standing maybe two feet from each other. Time seems to stand still for a moment, and then he raises the knife. As he does, I send my knee barreling up into him with all the force I can muster.

Right between his legs.

Doubling over with pain, Tony's face flushes to a deep shade of red as I drop to the ground beside Bruce to give Morton a clear shot. A single shot rings out, and I watch as a red dot appears in the center of Tony's forehead. He seems to stare at me for a moment before the life fades from his eyes. Then he lands crashing onto the ground right beside me.

    His face is positioned directly next to mine as we lie there on the ground beside one another. His eyes are still open, but there is nothing behind them anymore. No anger, no amusement, no mystery. Nothing. What once was there has vanished in an instant and all that's left is a lifeless corpse lying beside me.

    I hear the sound of sirens approaching in the distance, not far from here. Before I know it the sirens are right outside our house and the sound of many heavy footsteps come rushing in through the front door.

Chapter Fifty-Two
Bruce

Seven months later...

Eight broken ribs, a broken nose, a broken jawbone, and a concussion. That was the result of being punched and crushed between a massive man and a wall. I knew I was hurt when he slammed me up against the wall as I held onto his back, but I didn't know he'd managed to do that much damage.

But I'm alive, and more importantly, my wife and daughter are alive, so I don't have anything to complain about. Truly, I feel more fortunate than I ever have as I lie in bed and stare out at the sun as it rises in the sky. I've been waking up so early ever since it happened. I guess I feel like I'm afraid of wasting anymore time. Life is so short, even if everything goes right, and I don't want to squander a minute of it.

Judy sleeps soundly beside me. Life is good again. And best of all, there won't be any worry about Tony coming back. He's gone, and this time for good.

I can't say I feel like I was much of a hero, though. I tried to be, but it didn't work out that way. I suppose life is like that. It is always throwing curveballs at you. Judy and Annie both *act* like I'm a hero, but I think they might be trying to make me feel better. At least I tried my best, I guess, even if it didn't work out exactly how I'd planned. I imagined myself being like a hero in one of those old western movies, showing up and saving the day, but that didn't happen. Still, I put up a good fight for my family.

And one way or another, we got through it. We put up a fight, and we didn't back down in the face of violence. And I owe a lot to Lieutenant Morton. As far as I'm concerned, he deserves free rounds for life at the bar. Fortunately for my wallet, however, he quit drinking last year. And even if he hadn't, I don't think he'd accept more than a couple beers from me. According to him, he was just doing his job, nothing more. But I still feel like I honestly owe everything to him.

Things got back to normal relatively quickly after it happened. It was hectic for a while, to say the least, and after two months Judy and I decided to sell the house because we still felt disturbed about what had happened in it. There was something creepy about the fact that Tony had taken his last breath at the top of the staircase. I'm not a particularly superstitious man, and I don't believe in ghosts, but I still didn't like the memories of that whenever I would walk down the hallway in the middle of the night towards the bathroom. Each time I would pass the spot the memories would come back to me – the sight of him lying there on the ground, dead.

So we listed the house and fortunately it sold after a month. We moved across the Golden Gate Bridge into Marin County. I still commute most days into the city, but I also spend quite a bit of time in my home office. And here we've got greenery right outside our front door, which is a stark difference to our neighborhood in San Francisco. While I wouldn't call our neighborhood rural by any means, we live in a tranquil spot at the top of a hill. The house isn't big, by any means, but it's good for two people, and it's got a guest bedroom for Annie. She visits us often, but most of the time she is down in LA, busy with school. I'm so proud of her, and so is Judy.

    Slowly, I get out of bed and walk quietly to the kitchen, not wanting to wake Judy. Not yet, at least. I've gotten into the habit of fixing breakfast for us lately. Before, she would usually be the one to fix breakfast, but I figured it was time for me to start returning the favor, especially since I've been waking up so early. I'm not much in the way of a cook, but I can fix some good bacon, eggs, and biscuits, and sometimes I'll even try my hand at making pancakes.

    I stand in the kitchen with my eyes moving from the cupboard to the refrigerator, wondering if eggs or pancakes sounds better for today. My eyes swivel back towards the cupboard and I open it, pull out the box of flour and set it up on the counter beside the sugar jar. Pancakes it is. I whip them up as I play soft jazz music – that's another thing I've gotten in the habit of lately, as it seems to set a relaxing mood for the day.

    There is something funnily therapeutic about this routine to me, whether I'm frying up eggs and bacon or making pancakes. There is something nice about the calmness of the morning as I stand there behind the stove preparing our meal. It's a new feeling, as I never really felt this way before, and it's been like this ever since it all ended with Tony. As silly as it may sound, I guess the whole nightmare ordeal we went through as a family made me appreciate the little things in life more than I ever imagined I could. I don't want to take anything for granted anymore, not while I'm here with my family in good health, safe and secure.

When I finish the pancakes, I bring both plates on a big tray to the bedroom. Then I sit down beside Judy and rest the tray on our lap. I gently run a finger along her cheek. She stirs softly, then cracks an eye open. Her lips curve into a warm smile of recognition.

"Good morning," she says sleepily, letting out a little yawn.

"Morning. I hope you're hungry."

She sniffs the air and her eyes widen. She rubs them with her fingers and yawns again. "Oh, this smells and looks wonderful. Thanks, hon. You've become quite the breakfast chef."

"It's only pancakes." I chuckle.

"Even so, it's nice, and it tastes delicious." She pauses to take a sip of orange juice before playfully adding, "And you being the one to cook them gives me a few more minutes of extra sleep. You know I love my sleep."

I lean over to kiss her and then we pick up our forks and dig in as the sun begins to beam in through the window.

It's shaping up to be a perfect day.

Chapter Fifty-Three
Annie

It's a bright, sunny Friday afternoon in Southern California, and I've just finished classes for the day. Lately most things in life have felt like smooth sailing. I've made new friends on campus, joined some extracurricular groups, and have set several big goals for myself to accomplish over the next few years. One of those goals is to learn as much as possible about engineering. As a kid, I never thought I would want to go into engineering, but over the last few months the field has become pretty interesting to me. But I've got plenty of time to decide on a major, because I'm still only a freshman. Who knows what I'll end up doing? Maybe I'll wind up working on film sets or something unexpected like that. After all, I am living in Los Angeles, so why not? At this point, I feel like I'm ready for whatever the future might throw my way.

I feel good about how things are shaping up for me, and I think that if I manage to keep myself focused, I'll accomplish my goals. I talk to Mom and Dad all the time on the phone, and they come down to visit me once every couple of months, or sometimes every month. I drive up to Northern California pretty often, too, but most of the time I stick around here because I've got so many things that are keeping me busy, like studying and whatnot. I've also developed a pretty fun pastime of driving around LA and getting to know the city quite well. I like to cruise up on

Mulholland Drive and look down at the vastness of the city. It's a beautiful, winding road with so many scenic lookout points.

Things have been peaceful for me over the last seven months, and I'm hoping that trend continues. I don't see why it wouldn't. Ever since he left the picture, things have gone back to normal. I wish he could have found some way to get the help he needed, but it didn't work out that way.

I think about those final moments of that stressful period of time pretty often, but it doesn't bother me anymore. Not much, at least. And the memories never really give me any nightmares. Sometimes I just remember it all, starting from the beginning, back when we thought he was a tour guide and nothing more. It's wild to think about how it all happened, but it's history now, and he can't come after us anymore.

I still can't believe he tried to come after us in the first place, but I guess from his warped perspective, it made sense. I guess he felt like he had nothing to lose and wanted to get revenge on us, particularly my parents, for what he felt they had done to him. Seven years in prison and a dead brother. In his eyes, it was all their fault, and to an extent, mine.

I can't seem to do anything other than shake my head when I think about it, like right now as I sit on the patio of the coffee shop in Santa Monica and look out at the busy street. It's almost five o'clock, and people are finishing up with work for the week. I'm looking forward to a relaxing weekend myself. Heather is coming down from Northern California tomorrow and is going to spend Saturday and Sunday with me in LA. I haven't seen her in a while and I'm sure we will have a fun time together.

Mom and Dad were talking to me a week or two ago about planning a possible trip to New York. I think they expected me to be a little shocked about the idea, but it didn't bother me at all. They said it might be a way to bring us full closure as a family – to visit New York and for once have a fun, safe trip together without anything out of the ordinary happening. I told them it sounded good to me, as long as they promise me one thing: they do not, under any circumstances, hire a tour guide.

We all got a good laugh out of that. And of course, it was all in good fun. Dad said he'd get in touch with me again and work out the dates before we booked the plane tickets. I think he and Mom are right about it being a good idea, and a way to bring us full closure. I already feel closure, but it would be nice to go back to the place where all this began and have a good, *normal* family trip together. A trip where nothing insane happens.

That's what we went there for in the first place, after all.

After finishing my coffee, I stroll down Santa Monica Boulevard towards the beach. I don't have anything planned for the evening, and I think strolling along the sand and watching the sunset sounds like a perfect way to end the day.

A while later, I pass a family of four being shown the sights of downtown Santa Monica by an enthusiastic tour guide. For a second, I worry that all those bad memories might come flooding back into my mind and give me a surge of anxiety, but they don't. In fact, I realize now that I'm having a hard time even remembering Tony's face. It was thin, I remember, but I don't remember many other details. Did he have blue eyes, or were they brown?

I shake my head, chuckle, and feel myself smiling. I can't even remember him that well. He's fading away, and so is the fear I once felt. He's disappearing from my mind.

All those bad memories are just that – *memories*. Nothing more. And those memories can never hurt me.

The End

Other thriller books by Nash Greene
The Lying Husband
The Jealous Roommate
The Husband's Secretary
The Jealous Doctor
The Regular Customer
She Saw Everything
Her Boyfriend's Past
The Husband's Deceit

Printed in Dunstable, United Kingdom

80038826R00167